Her Tower of Babel

Unless the LORD builds the House...

DAPHNE BALINDA

WESTBOW
PRESS®
A DIVISION OF THOMAS NELSON
& ZONDERVAN

WestBow Press books may be ordered through booksellers or by contacting:

WestBow Press
A Division of Thomas Nelson & Zondervan
1663 Liberty Drive
Bloomington, IN 47403
www.westbowpress.com
844-714-3454

ISBN: 978-1-6642-4112-1 (sc)
ISBN: 978-1-6642-4111-4 (e)

Print information available on the last page.

WestBow Press rev. date: 08/23/2021

For my children

Danielle, Arnold, and Trudy
Danielle for your great insights, colorful imagination, and editing this book;
Arnold for affection and great humor; and
Trudy Joan for bringing us great joy, amazing faith, and inspiring miracles.

Much love and thanks to:

God for giving me inspiration to write this book, my children and settling
me into a family that inspired great spiritual transformation.

My parents: My parents, Tetete and Abwooli for teaching me to love and fear
God; my godmother, Akiiki Gertrude for active guidance and friendship.
My confidant and mentor Gilbert, and all my loving siblings, cousins, nieces, and nephews,
and godchildren, for constant reminders that I am loved, accepted, and valued.
My prayer warriors and friends that stick closer than family: Sheila, Esther, Viona,
Tabitha, Diane, Carole, Ama, Esperance, Violet, Bubu, Marie-Paule, Rogers, Paul, and
Rosemary, for teaching me about friendship, and encouraging me in my faith:
Daniel, Rogers, Charlie, Molly for fun times and believing in me, teaching me to journal.
Chrissie Wells and Julie Keys for fun Bible study sessions.
Spiritual mentors: Pastor Ama, Pastor Gichora, and Pastor
Wanje for holding my hand in spiritual growth.
Theodore Kirunda for prayers, encouragement, and book cover design.

THE TOWER OF BABEL

Genesis 11:1-8 MSG

"At one time, the whole Earth spoke the same language. It so happened that as they moved out of the east, they came upon a plain in the land of Shinar and settled down.

3 They said to one another, "Come, let's make bricks and fire them well." They used brick for stone and tar for mortar.

4 Then they said, "Come, let's build ourselves a city and a tower that reaches Heaven. Let's make ourselves famous so we won't be scattered here and there across the Earth."

5 God came down to look over the city and the tower those people had built.

6-9 God took one look and said, "One people, one language; why, this is only a first step. No telling what they'll come up with next—they'll stop at nothing! Come, we'll go down and garble their speech so they won't understand each other." Then God scattered them from there all over the world. And they had to quit building the city. That's how it came to be called Babel because there God turned their language into "babble." From there God scattered them all over the world."

FOREWORD

This book shows how brokenness can lead to self-deception and bondage, and one woman's journey to freedom. It is a testimony that God will stand behind those who believe and trust Him to intervene no matter how far from the course they have veered. Redemption comes when the veil is lifted and courage borne of faith triumphs.

This is a voice of understanding and encouragement for those who are in abusive relationships, feeling entrapped and afraid and thinking that there is no way out.

For those who have enthroned marriage, family, children, and wealth above God. They lie and cheat to get and maintain relationships that do not honor God's purposes. They built monuments in their honor, thus worshipping the created rather than the creator, giver, and sustainer.

For those who think they are worshipping God the creator but have inadvertently made a god of convenience. A god who does not interfere with their choices. The one who turns a blind eye to a life of debauchery, cheating, perverting the innocent, blasphemy, dishonoring their parents.

INTRODUCTION

Xandra desired to build a family of her dreams with a gorgeous, hardworking, and sophisticated husband. She met Sean who thought, felt, and desired the same as he; adored and esteemed her. They both admired good manners, intelligence, and well-groomed children; a partnership in wealth and prosperity; a family that prayed together, traveled the world and was happy, devoid of strife. It was a perfect set up and achievable by her standards and ability. She was born in the Catholic faith and knew what had to be done to live a good and perfect life. She had explored various religions and new age philosophies in her search for spiritual fulfillment.

Sean's demands were for an ideal family with a beautiful home, an obedient and adoring wife, impeccably mannered and excellently groomed children; honor, respect, and admiration of peers. He desired a kind of wife who could kneel to serve him. He did not find one, but many, and none of them could give him the one hundred percent he craved. Sean professed to believe in God but did not think God had anything to do with how he lived his life. He prayed when he needed God and thanked him for what he achieved. The evidence of God's pleasure in him was his wealth.

Xandra and Sean who got into a union according to their principles – the end justifies the means; the sky would be the limit. They assumed God had rubber-stamped their dream. They had realistic goals and focus but made up the rules as they went. The relationship though romanticized, required deception and lies to be engaged, and the consequences were: people got hurt, unconventional covenants made, chronic infidelity tolerated, money replaced love and presence, legal procedures sneered on, and worship of God mocked. The appearance of a perfect family was upheld as the most important above genuine inter-personal relationships within. Fear ruled, propagated by control through intimidation, manipulation, and abuse. Xandra Rafiq and Sean Cato came together in their brokenness and built a relationship on the sand. They started united in the plan. They were going to make an enviable lifestyle and they would be unstoppable - heaven on earth. Then communication failed, the vision became blurred, and the tower came tumbling on down. Who will survive?

This shows how people that are consumed with achievement lose focus of what matters most – their eternal soul and family. Some people are like a race car driver who enjoys accelerating, misses the warning sign until he finds himself flying off a precipice. So do many women hold onto relationships that are detrimental to their spirituality and physical safety. While their children hurt, or commit suicide, or fall away to addictions. Civic leaders hold onto power with popular policies that keep them in power rather than benefit the citizens. They legislate laws that promote promiscuity and idolatry; hinder discipline of the young by parents and teachers in a society that continues to grow amorphous in our global village. Individual achievements keep people in denial about their lack of fulfillment - closeness to God. They work and party harder to make up for the lack of any kind of habit that puts them in proximity with God, their spouse, or family and community. Achievement becomes the new identity as everything is for the glory of the individual. Xandra Rafiq, Sean Cato, and their children each took up an interest that binds them to separate communities in which each group has its own unique belief, culture, rules, customs, and even language. So as with the tower of Babel, family members live in such diverse worlds that they cannot relate or understand each other. Can Xandra gain her freedom from fear, abuse, and emptiness, and save her children?

God, in His grace, is not going to leave you, your marriage, your family, and your friendships in the scattered, dis-connected condition that they may be in. God in his grace is not going to leave you with a language barrier keeping you from Him and those you love. He desires to prosper you, with hope and a future. He wants you to be one with Himself and one with the most important people in your life but you must commit all your plans to Him then He alone will give you the desires of your heart.

PROLOGUE

"I was heartbroken, scared, I had a lot of anxiety; I was worried, I felt weak, and I had no idea how I was ever going to come up with the strength. But I just closed my eyes and took a blind leap. I knew I had to get out of there."

- Bob Casey, Jr.

"*When a relationship, involving children, has deteriorated from unpleasant to unacceptable how does one end it? I have lost my identity, self-esteem, and moral campus. When and how does one without an alternative source of income get out of this mess? How did I allow myself to join the statics of abused women? I gave this man the best years of my life.*" Xandra coiled herself further into a fetal position as she wept. The pain felt physical. It stretched from her throat, through her heart, and into her gut and she could not vomit it out. She was weeping so hard she wasn't even aware she was breathing. She was not sure if it was purely hurt, shame, fear, or all of it, but she knew that her life had come crushing and she had to face it. "*Who on earth did I marry? What a fool I have been to adore, honor, and tolerate his infidelity?*" She allowed the bitter tears of fear, the years of trying hard, and enduring abuse; patching things up, emotional neglect, and physical abandonment; rejection, betrayal, and criticisms; restraints, control, and loneliness; prayers unanswered, and long periods of fasting that didn't pay off. She moaned, "Oh God, where are you? O LORD, help me! Help me!" Still prideful, she struggled with the thought that her housekeeper could walk in on her and see her vulnerability. She was thankful that the children were at school, therefore she had time to herself. She nearly broke down as she drove them to school, strained, forcing smiles and looking normal. Funny that through it all she was still too proud to show her pain. She couldn't even call her buddies or a prayer partner to cry with her or hold her in her pain. She still had a prayer. "God, help me" she pleaded amidst the sobs. This was her problem to fix and she didn't have a game plan. "*If dad was alive. He would listen to me and tell me what to do. I cannot tell mom. She will panic and tell me what I do not want to hear, whatever it may be.*" She knew without a doubt that she had had enough of the endless cycle of try and fail, fear, and uncertainty, and she couldn't go on as before. Her decision was one of life and death and only she could make that. She would Xandra it if a friend she loved tried to reason with her to continue in this relationship for any reason. She wailed some more. Glad to have the tears rolling and her abs able to push the pain in breaths out she started to enjoy it and didn't want to stop.

Xandra uncoiled herself slowly, stretching out her limbs and rolled onto her stomach then rolled over to her knees dreading to get up. Intending to pray away her pain, she wondered "what do I look like after such a heavy outpouring of tears and facial contortions?" She got up and staggered slowly to the dressing mirror and checked her face. A feeling of self-pity swept over her and she grimaced with pain and the tears started flowing again. This time she watched herself as she cried. She felt as ugly as she looked in that mirror and that made her sadder and humored her too. She couldn't help smiling through the half-open eyes and pouting lips, with her head arched sideways. The focus was no longer on what had driven her to this point but what she looked like in grief. She laughed a little at first and then laughed hard.

"If only my mom and friends could see me now. I am like a baby!" She thought. What was that her friend said when she was in pain? "My heart is so sore.!" That seemed a fitting expression, but it was for the weak. She stood straight in that m*irror and decided she was not going to be a wimp* *but must stand strong and confident. "I wish I could cry with someone today. Pain is best savored alone to drain the septic wound without others trying to close it up to protect me. I'll tell them when I can laugh about it so I do not look pathetic, needy, and weak" Xandra resolved. "It is time to clean up and be me again. Record my misery; list my tears on your scroll -- are they not in your record" She pleaded from Psalm 56: 8.NIV*

1

Freedom is birthed in pain —

-Daphne Balinda

"How dare he threaten me? After all the years I have loved and tolerated his serial infidelity, control, abuse, criticism, mockery, manipulation and now he wants to rein me in further so I won't have friends and then don't even socialize? He is physically and emotionally unavailable. To what end? For how long am I going to live like this? It is like being in a box but one without ventilation. It is a death trap. He is proposing death to me. And he gives me an ultimatum – a choice between life and death because to continue in this marriage I have to accept his conditions or risk to be thrown out." Xandra prayed and pleaded with God for a decision on this. Deep inside she knew she wouldn't live this life anymore. Things had to change at all costs. But what did choosing her way mean when she did not have a job and had children's lives to consider?

Xandra sat in the chapel, content after taking the children to school, and prayed for a response to Sean, who had cautioned her to respond to him first thing in the morning before asking anyone for advice. She promised not to seek human advice and here she was, seeking divine wisdom. She got off her knees and sat on the sofa *thinking "If I concede to his demands it will get worse. I have given my all and he does not trust, love, and honor me. Sean is giving me an ultimatum to stop holding a monthly prayer group at home! How does one kick prayer out of home? He wants me to seek permission to fast, to attend any retreat or training, and report every meeting I attend.* Xandra felt bile rise in her gut as she remembered the demands. "You must ask for permission to visit even if you say she is sick. It is disrespectful to just decide you have to rush to see her. It does not go well with me for you to business because you have to sometimes meet with men and I do not trust you. My wife will not be employed by another. And those people you call friends, you must leave them because they are not approved by the family." Xandra had listened without interruption, knowing she did not agree but was not going to argue about it all. *"Who does he take me for? A child? Do I have to permit him when he travels to spend time nursing his mother?"* She argued silently as he talked on and on. "I do not agree with our housekeeper disciplining the children. She has no right and you must expel her." Xandra could no longer control herself. "What? Mavis has been with us for ten years and loves our children. She has never abused them but lovingly guided them and now you want us to just get rid of her? Well, she works for me and I will not let her go." Sean had gone silent, then hang up. Remembering this exchange just brought back more of her grievances. *"Sean wants me to get the approval of the entire family approval regarding my hairstyle. I bet he is jealous of my fitness and has commanded that I unsubscribe from Crossfit to join any other gym of his choice. He has never read a report card, or spoken to the children about God; he dares to tell them that they should not go to church and listen to preachers telling them who and what they can be. For that damage alone I cannot have him in my life. Doesn't the Bible say such a person is better off thrown drowning with rocks tied around his neck? Forgive me for the thought, LORD. But, he has crossed a line to undermine the faith of my children, just to hurt me. LORD, won't you do something about it? He has proposed to turn the children into Muslims. The children are already asking for their right to choose if they go to church or not. LORD, all the work of disciplining my children is being undone. I held on to this marriage for their sake and now*

I am losing them to the darkness. LORD, do you want me to wallow in a polygamous marriage? He has threatened to hurt me physically if I confront him about his extramarital relationships. How long shall I pay for my poor choices LORD?" She complained in prayer and came close to calling fire down from heaven on Sean. Xandra fell to her knees wailing, *"LORD, don't you love me anymore? Will you not intervene and help me because I have failed in my wisdom and strength. Everything I have tried to do has crumbled. I know your way is a sure deal. Help me. Help me. I pray and counsel others and their prayers are heard. Now Sean mocks me saying even God won't hear you because your prayers are not right. And I tell console others saying God will rescue you and help you but they look on me wondering what did she do to suffer so?"* A heatwave of anger rose in her to replace helplessness and she turned her thoughts to God in a plea *"for how long my LORD shall I put up with this? I have honored this man, loved him, raised our children, and waited for affection but got criticism on criticism and now more restraint?"* She tried to be silent awhile for response and her mind wandered. *"I know that long after God has forgiven me I shall pay for the consequences of my sin. I did things my way and asked God to endorse them. I did not obey God and my parents and built a house on sand. BUT O God, in the name of Jesus, I have repented, won't you rescue me?"* And on and on she travailed for hours past the time she was to call Sean with her decision.

The train of self-deception moves fast and demands all your energy to hold on, wrap up, and strive to survive. If left to go for long it continues on the uncertain, indefinite, and obvious destination of destruction. The blessing is to know when to stop and get off, and the courage to jump off even if that means grave injury or death. Experiencing difficulty and pain can be a major blessing. It equips one to stand in the face of fear and make life-altering decisions in faith, with calm, poise, and certainty. *"I can't go on like this anymore. I don't want to live like this. I have been hanging onto this miserable marriage for the sake of my children. I was afraid that I can't afford to financially take care of them. Well, they are God's children. God loves them enough to protect and provide for them. If God has seen it fit for us to suffer lack or for Sean to steal them from me, I will still worship Him. I will not make them a battle issue. He can have them."* She resolved. *"I have hit rock bottom there is no further to go."* Xandra heard, an inaudible voice agreeing with her: "When you have come to the end of yourself, as many do, you meet God; the one you have been searching for. You look into His face and get to know Him. Then you will look around ashamedly for the god you had made and know that your understanding has heightened; your knowledge increased and finally you can walk in wisdom because you have found the All-wise, Almighty, All-knowing, Ever-present God."

When Xandra had prayed out all her complaints, pleas, and emotions and could cry no more, she lifted her face and looked around. Then she looked down at her hands. A feeling of calm swept over her. In her spirit, she knew it was going to be alright. It came at first as a thought *"if Jesus died to set captives free and you obey the oppressor then Jesus would have died for nothing."* She got up and sat down, grabbed her Bible, and phone at the same time because she knew this was in the Bible somewhere. She opened her phone to search "Jesus said I have come to set the captives free". And there it was, Isaiah 61 *The Spirit of the Sovereign LORD is on me because the LORD has anointed me to preach good news to the poor. He has sent me to bind up the brokenhearted, to proclaim freedom for the captives and release from darkness for the prisoners, to proclaim the year of the LORD's favor and the day of vengeance of our God, to comfort all who mourn,"* She searched further when Jesus read it in Luke 4:18 NIV, *"The Spirit of the Lord is on me because he has anointed me to proclaim good news to the poor. He has sent me to proclaim freedom for the prisoners and recovery of sight for the blind, to set the oppressed free, to proclaim the year of the Lord's favor."* Could the LORD, God, have spoken louder than that? Xandra was filled with excitement because she had found her divine wisdom. God has responded and now she could, without many words take a stand. For her to accept to live in oppression is death; it is to profess that Jesus died for nothing and her faith is for nothing. She could choose life or death. And if she leans on God, He will protect her. He will fulfill His promise. In the face of the threats of the unknown and roaring fear, Xandra would rather die in the arms of her savior. The veil was lifted, finally after 17 years of struggle. Now she had to break free of the chains that have bound her in misery for so long. She would die for her faith. She picked up her bags and headed home, praising God.

Twenty minutes later, she got home with her usual smile plastered on. She sat down in her comfortable seat and typed up Luke 4:18-19 NIV and sent it to Sean, adding "if I agree with your conditions then Christ would have died for nothing. I choose him." The Word of God makes the devil tremble. Sean had lost power and was now filled with fear because he started a tirade of abuse, criticism, and threats as they assailed him. All Xandra knew what to do was to stand. And she stood her ground. She resisted the devil and his roaring. Nothing else mattered now but her walk with Jesus. The message of salvation was clearer now than it had been since she was born. No one could explain it better than experience. The tower had fallen, and she had survived. She also knew very well that the battle for freedom was just beginning and it would be gruesome and there would be casualties. However, she had experienced that living a life of fear was not worth it all. Freedom at any cost had to be attained.

2

"It is for freedom that Christ has set us free. Stand firm, then, and do not let yourselves be burdened again by the yoke of slavery. — Galatians 5:13 NIV

Her mind was racing with new revelations. *"This is how entrapment works. Funny how one waits for years, blinded by gifts and intermittent tokens of affection. A switch from threats, criticism, and false promises knowing very well they are dealing with one who lies well. After knowing how he camouflages his true character and intentions; yet continuing to hope, fast, and pray for change. Can one pray to twist God's hand? And, I, knowing God has not endorsed things, pray some more and repent and anoint and make declarations and hang in for the sake of the children. But it has worked for many in the past and some are around me. Self-deception is the beginning of spiritual blindness. When the veil comes on, no one and nothing can help you out except the grace of God."* Xandra contemplated. Again she heard an inaudible response, "Samuel told Saul that to obey God is better than sacrifice. Good intentions will not move God while you are not obeying Him. Prayers and fasting will lift the veil so you can obey God, repent, and walk with Him to freedom." *"Do I stop praying now? If I knew how to undo the knots in my life, LORD, I would do it right away."*

Xandra decided to try once more to do what she used to do to clear her mind, take a jog, and run until her mind was clear. She put her earphones on and skimmed through her playlist and decided on something cheerful - "It's a beautiful day, the sun is shining …" by Micheal Buble. It gave the push to start jogging but then she did not listen after the first stanza as her thoughts raced faster. *I can't believe I gave my heart to someone so deceptive. But isn't this stupidity the cause of women's woes? Isn't this how we women support and propagate abuse and violence then cry foul? Why did I put up with him all these years? And the misuse of scripture that we hold onto telling us not to withhold sex back from each other because our bodies are not ours. Isn't that the devils' trap that keeps us vulnerable? He calls me regularly while away telling me how much he misses me and can't wait to see me. I work my expectations up expecting happy times with a husband who has been gone six weeks. When he arrives he first notices my chapped hands. He smiles and gives out lots of presents. He looks unimpressed with my food but keeps the peace. He walks around taking stock of the state of the home. Listens to the children's stories then retreats to his computer. He starts telling me about his business challenges and plans. He spends the first two days giving instructions to gardeners and fixing what he can. On the third night, he watches the news, retires to bed early, and withdraws to his messages on phone. When I get into the bed he ignores me while continues reading the news and later on when it suits me he wakes me up feigning much affectionate. After a night of passionately fulfilling conjugal rights, I dutifully get up early to attend to the children and happy to make him breakfast. When I come to get him for breakfast, he is rude and cold to me saying some bad thoughts about me crossed his mind. He spends the day criticizing everything I do and say, complaining about everything that is broken or not in place and my food. Then he starts picking on the children. The visit is over. Enters mister frost.* Xandra has by now run a kilometer in these thoughts and is now walking fast as the thoughts get heavy and emotions rise. *After a hellish day like that, without a nice word exchanged he waits in bed for me to come to bed and pulls me into an embrace to have sex. When I tell him I am not in the mood he insists I have to try and he will make it worthwhile. Not even the flu or headache will stop Sean. He persuades and grabs until I realize that the only way to keep the peace is to let him have his way. Then I do the usual, making excuses for my weaknesses. After all, he is keeping a roof over our heads, generous in maintaining us. I shall give it my best and make the sex worthwhile. When it is all done, I turn away disgusted with myself. Is this not prostitution? Is this not what prostitutes do to make a living – have sex for food and clothing and care of their children?* Xandra did not even realize it but she had stopped walking and is staring at a bush but not even seeing it. She was not aware of which music was playing. The pain and shame and disgust and anger are overwhelming. Xandra remembered the people she loved and trusted. Sometimes the people that love us can give dumb advice because they want to protect us. Their advice could entrench one deeper into bondage and you have to suffer the consequences of those decisions. She thought of four years ago when she confided in friends and family that she was done living in polygamy and would never get intimate with Sean again. She got alarmed remarks like "If you refuse to have sex with a man he will kill you. It is the worst thing you can do to him." Another one said "he is the father of your children, what is the point of refusing him. It is just sex after all." Yet another strategized with an African saying interpreted "A man loves his children because of their mother's crotch. For the sake of your children, endure it all." Being strong-willed, she argued that she won't accept. Her immediate family at first congratulated her for coming out of living in sin. When the going got tough and Sean was withholding maintenance some told her "he is the father of your children. Drop the matter, forgive him for the sake of your children. Wait until they are older then you can decide." Mhh, *While compromising with the devils' wiles to save my children I am losing them to him! I tolerated all the wrongs for the sake of my children and now I am losing them. They are angry at the injustices they have witnessed and heard, and cannot understand why their mother is taking it. My children are rebelling against me because they are feeling unprotected; I can't fight for myself. They say they do not see what I pray so much for and God does not hear me. This is not what I want to teach my children,"* Xandra moaned. She had affirmed to her family "If I die, I die. This is a matter of life and death mommy. The LORD is my Shepherd. If I continue to live under this oppression, it means I do not trust Him to be my helper, and then my faith is worth nothing. What use is God to me if I cannot trust Him?" Her mother knew better than to argue. *Well, if God allows him to hurt me or kill me then it is for the better. If God allows him to abandon us with the children, He will make a way for our provision. If God allows Sean to take the children from me, He will take good care of them because He loves them too, and He will make a way for me.* This last thought lifted her. At this memory, Xandra snapped back to the moment, and she started jogging again. She remembered a favorite scripture in Psalm 46 NIV– she had memorized parts of it "God is my refuge. God is my strength. An ever-present help in trouble. Therefore, I will not fear, though the earth be removed, and all the mountains are cast into the midst of the sea…"

This fear and endurance that is cultivated and churned out to wives and daughters is part of the reason so many narcissistic men are killing women. Violence against women is propagated by socialization first at home and then the global culture of sexual freedom and materialism, misinterpretation and misuse of scripture, and failure of society to take into account narcissism. Narcissism is self-love at the expense of others and sickness at any level to be treated like HIV/AIDS and Covid-19. This is all rooted in the absence of love. Xandra stopped to catch her breath. She was getting excited too. *"What a revelation! I have to run home and blog about it. I am going to fight for women and be part of the movement that fights against violence. But the boys have to be nurtured. I shall make it a prayer point too."* She walked all the way home feeling wiser, thinking of ways to help other women. She resolved to sensitize men and women against violence and marital rape and narcissism and all forms of abuse against women and children and the vulnerable. *"First, I am going to divorce this man, and trust God to use me to lift and guide others in the same predicament. There is purpose in my trials after all."*

3

"Will you walk into my parlor?" said the Spider to the Fly, "'Tis the prettiest little parlor that ever you did spy; The way into my parlor is up a winding stair, And I've a many curious things to shew when you are there."

By Mary Howitt

It was not love at first sight. Xandra was out to flirt and not to have a relationship. Sean was an attractive, 43 years old. Tall, slim, and dark exotic complexion. He was always dressed formally in the daylight hour and did not wear a wedding ring. Xandra was an beautiful, in her early 30s and unattached. Their attraction to each other was mutual, with interest in first-rate lifestyles. They loved vintage wine, fine dining, dance, and travels promised years of fun. They were both ambitious, goal-oriented, intelligent, sophisticated, well-traveled, and proud. They both believed in the "end deserves the means". They looked good together and that was a good binding factor. She was good for his image and he called her "my gift from God." She thought he was a doting father and a very caring and gentle person who would be an excellent husband if loved right.

According to mutual friends, Sean was an astute businessman and very generous. She believed in investing wisely and of course, she would partner with Sean, under his expert guidance to grow her investments. Xandra went to church on Sunday, just enough not to make Sean feel uncomfortable. Drinking alcohol and premarital sex was not prohibited by her church. She was young, pliable. Sean believed everyone had a price and even though Xandra was playing hard to get, he would persist and mold her into what he wanted.

There were good and wise friends who wanted to conduct due diligence on Sean but Xandra couldn't hear of it. Eva Njeri, her cousin, advised her to stay away from Sean because he was still married, and had children which would complicate things. On another occasion, Eva confronted Xandra and told her to take it slow. "At least play dentist, have fun until he has sorted his marital situation. What if they have a chance to reconcile, where will that leave you?" "Playing dentist" insinuated flirting with a guy and letting him meet all the costs of the outings, then ditch him without having sex. Having him pay your dating bills would by synonymous with pulling out one's teeth. Xandra was horrified at the thought because she was earning and the idea of using a man like that was inconceivable. She broke ties with Eva for a long time and did not confide in her anymore.

Assured she knew how to manage life without outside influence, Xandra dug in. "There is a way that appears to be right, but in the end, it leads to death." Proverbs 14:12

4

Truth or reality is avoided when it is painful. We can revise our maps only when we have the discipline not to avoid the pain. To have such discipline, we must be totally dedicated to the truth, not partially. That is to say, we must always hold truth, as best as we can determine it, to be more crucial, more vital to our self-interest, than our comfort. Conversely, we must always consider our personal discomfort relatively unimportant, and, indeed, even welcome it in the service of the search for truth. Mental health is an ongoing process of dedication to reality at all costs. What does this life of total dedication to the truth mean? It means, above all, a life of continuous and never-ending stringent self-examination and honesty with oneself - Scott Peck

At a consultation meeting with her Pastor Thea Jones, Xandra did not hesitate to get to the heart of what irked her today. "where do I begin, Pastor Jones? I confess that I sold my soul to attain romance, family, and keep a man. It didn't take exchange of money, vows, or any satanic acts but I turned my eyes from the LORD. It has cost me greatly. Getting back on track and gaining my freedom is costing me much." Xandra suppressed a sob, "I was born and raised in a decent Catholic family. I was baptized at two months of age and confirmed after catechism at age 10 years. I had a strong will, hot temper, and much pride but usually very well-mannered and that helped get away with naughtiness. I realized at a very young age that I couldn't confess the truth to the priest but felt guilty enough before God. By the time I was 13 years old, I had quit on the sacrament of confession. While in college, I linked up with some very calm friends who took me to Pentecostal youth fellowship. I got saved and felt the most peace at that time. I got to read the Bible for the first time. I gave away my mirror and all the dresses I wore to go to the disco. I avoided my partying friends to the best of my ability because I knew that I was vulnerable to fall." Xandra smiled and went silent for a few minutes relishing the memory. Pastor Jones coughed to draw her attention and urge her on. She was a good listener. Xandra trusted her and enjoyed talking to her. Xandra continued to bare her memories unloading her guilt, shame and feeling true this once. After all, she didn't have to keep up appearances. "The daily temptations in college were so many. The girls in the hostel would just introduce their male friends to a pretty girl just to get an outing, knowing fully well that the girl was not available. Such a guy was always sleazy and out for quick gain and the girls outsmarted him and labeled him a "square". I don't know the origins of this label but it obviously insinuated that the dude was predictable and not very smart. And O the fun stories on the weekend of who fooled who and who got away! I didn't miss the outings much because as much as I enjoyed the discotheque there was always the nagging fear that the rapture would find me there and I would be left behind. One Sunday morning while nursing a hangover a roommate told me that it was called "Catholic guilt". I agreed with her but it didn't make it any better." Pastor Jones sipped on her bottle of water as Xandra continued to relate her journey taken up by the memories and almost forgetting where she was at. It was a captivating and revealing story because Pastor Jones looked captivated. "I was introduced to the Pentecostal Church on Milton Road where I accepted my first Altar call. It was exciting and I looked forward to the journey. Sadly, when I got back to college campus all I heard all week were plans for Friday and I knew that I would go out. I always accepted to go dancing on Friday night and drank enough to keep me sick in bed on Saturday. This went on for 6 consecutive weeks of taking the Altar call on Sunday and backsliding by mid-week. My closest friend, Annette, told me that I had backslid so many times I was not crawling on my butt. She was right." The phone rang and Pastor Jones excused herself to pick it. Xandra realized she had taken a lot of time and needed to leave for her next errand. She stood up abruptly, picking her bag and walking around the sofa waiting for the call to end so she can excuse herself and leave. Pastor Jones put the phone down and looked affectionately at Xandra with a finger in the air.

"Xandra, that was a very active and interesting youth, but you know that God loves you so much to keep drawing you to Himself. He is giving you the last laugh against temptation." She paused for a moment gazing at the window, then noted "did you know that you would make a good life coach and counselor? Perhaps that is one of your callings. Who better to talk to the youth, mothers, and wives with your track record?" She looked seriously at Xandra and they both burst out laughing as they walked to the door.

Xandra had separated from Beau two years before meeting Sean and was in the process of divorce. Divorcing Beau on grounds of infidelity, psychological abuse and desertion. She could never imagine Sean capable of infidelity when he was so straight and devoted to her. Beau had been her best friend and mentor for five years before they decided to get married. They knew each other so well that Xandra was convinced marrying Beau was a bad idea because of his control issues and temper. Beau loved and dotted on Xandra and didn't want to lose her even though he was averse to marriage. He knew that marriage was the only way to hold onto her. Xandra was afraid to let her friend down and frankly, she didn't know if she could be anything or do anything well without him. Against the advice of colleagues and intimate friends, Xandra agreed to marry Beau, justifying it with "if it doesn't work we can always divorce." The foundation of this house was sand and when the storm of infidelity hit, five months after the wedding, it crumbled like a pack of cards.

5

"All men should strive to learn before they die, what they are running from, and to, and why." - James Thurber

At the time of meeting Sean, Xandra was employed as a Project Manager with the United Nations Development Programme in South Africa, and she loved it. She had diplomatic privileges, a good salary, and career opportunities for advancement. She had saved and was buying properties, a dream she had conceived as a young girl. She knew she didn't have time to start a family, but she yearned for companionship and was aware that at thirty-two years she was running out of time. *"If only I could find a guy who earns less than me so I can marry him and ask him to stay at home and take care of our kids while I work,"* she thought. She despised the powerlessness of the wife who stayed home and believed every woman should go to work. Xandra knew very well what her heart's desires were and she was going to search and make it happen. Only she believed in that fallacy. What she desired most was the inverted role of being the husband with her man playing mommy and wife. Now, this was a prodigious vision for a high-flying executive. Xandra had become a scattergood whose imaginations, dreams, and ambitions trumped good advice of well-intentioned loved ones.

Xandra's childhood dream was to walk down the aisle in a wedding gown and have two children. She dreamed of being a wife who served her husband and dotted on her children. She fantasized about the meals she would make, the romance that would never end, and a man that idolized her enough to never cheat or abuse her in any way. Even as she made plans to be a husband, she desired to be married to a strong character, a protective and handsome man. Xandra had hit a conundrum of cognitive dissonance. She was in a world of her own making and not even her most intimate friends and closest family could understand her. She was not seeking anyone's advice or taking opinion anyway. It is hard to tell how it could be possible to be one person with conflicting desires when one doesn't even know that brought on the internal inconsistency that made her squirm. Could this explain why she couldn't let her guard down with her colleagues and made those her friends then retired home through the gym to an empty house? Needless to say, Xandra went to the gym at six o'clock every morning and again at six o'clock in the evening. She felt lonely but not enough to do anything about it because she did not think there was anything wrong with her. She resorted to having meetings over coffee in the cafeteria and made sure she paid the entire bill to avoid owing anyone anything, and in case the opposite sex tried to take advantage. She hanged with guys a lot more than women because the men did not pry as much as the women would. Besides the women, she had tried to hang-out with, warned her that she would be taken advantage of and her reputation would suffer if she was seen around the guys often. Xandra did not care for this advice because she believed in herself and that is all that mattered. She played hard to get and remained mysterious because she never talked about herself much, no one was invited to her house, as she never visited any of her friends or colleagues' homes either.

Xandra and her ex-husband, Beau, had mutually agreed to divorce and they maintained their friendship. Although she trusted in Beau's wisdom, she did not take his advice to take her time before committing to this relationship. He gave her one last piece of advice on their last phone conversation, "do not quit working, pursue further education and career advancement, Xandra."

She did not hesitate to tell him that Sean was special. She retorted "I believe Sean is the only man that I have met and felt he met the criteria to be a prospective father of my children. I can tell because of his perfect smooth fingers and feet". Beau laughed nervously and concluded, "Well, congratulations my dear. It is time for some of us to go earn our bacon."

Even as Xandra put the phone down, she knew Sean was right but did not want to believe it. Beau was always a voice of reason, but she desperately wanted to have what she believed Sean could offer her.

Listen to advice and accept discipline, and at the end, you will
be counted among the wise. -Proverbs 19:20 NIV

6

"You don't love someone for their looks, or their clothes, or for their fancy car, but because they sing a song only you can hear." -Oscar Wilde

As Xandra rounded the corner to her office, she caught glimpse of a group of people surrounding her office seemingly admiring something. She walked over past the colleagues and stood still at the sight of the three most beautiful, huge flower arrangements on a three-tier stand. The curiosity of her colleagues was at its peak because no one knew she had any love interests in her life. Xandra was more embarrassed than excited because she wanted to keep this affair secret so she didn't have to explain who her Sean was. And if she mentioned his name, someone might know him and tell search and give her information she was not ready to receive. She pretended she did not know who it was. Eunice her assistant, picked the card and asked her to open she Xandra feigned any knowledge of who it was. The card was signed Sean, and now curiosity grew. Someone showed the basket that came with the flowers – under normal circumstances a girl would be flattered but the embarrassment was too much to handle. Xandra pretended disinterest and irritation. She stared at the flowers feigning confusion and displeasure. The heat was building in her body. She took off her coat and hang it on the back of her seat and sat down to work so everyone could take a cue and leave. Xandra's conscience was not clear. She squirmed for a few minutes then picked up the phone and called Sean, not to thank him but to tell him off.

Sean picked up the phone with calm confidence, "Hello, Hello, Xandra I am so glad you called." Xandra couldn't restrain herself "Hello, Sean. I have just received a big surprise in my office and I believe it is from you." She paused. Sean giggled. Xandra continued, sounding officious, "thank you for the thought but please do not do this ever again because it has caused me a lot of embarrassment and raised suspicion in my workplace. I like to keep my private life to myself." Sean politely noted, "I am sorry to embarrass you, but I cannot promise not to do that again." Xandra was incensed at his stubborn attitude but excited by it at the same time. She didn't take Sean to be the stubborn type because he was always very gentle and soft-spoken with everyone. She thought she would overpower him. Deep inside she admired a man who had a stronger will than her. She had met her match.

She was still not sure how far to take this relationship. She was sure that she would take her time, and when she decided to go all the way with Sean they would first medical tests. Xandra believed this would be a major test of Sean's seriousness. When Sean picked her up for a day at the Hartbeespoort dam, she was all smiles and beautifully made up. She wore a white dress, tucked in at the waist with buttons running down from the neck to the navel, and a blue and white checkered jersey slang over her shoulders. She was wearing Linda McCartney sandals with a matching black leather satchel across her shoulders. She looked ravishing and his eyes showed his admiration. He walked over to her side, opened the car door. She swung both legs into the car. Her dress lifted a little to show the soft part above her knee. She didn't intend to show skin but that unintentional flirt got Sean hesitating to close her door for a few seconds and she knew without a doubt that she had him nailed. She loved the feeling of the power of Sean.

"Where are we going this time?" asked Xandra. Sean looking amused responded, "I am kidnapping you from your world of all work and no play." The sound of that statement made her heart leap with excitement. She teasingly leaned over and extended both her wrists towards him "you forgot to handcuff me." Sean extended his left hand and interlaced his fingers with her right hand declaring "the day is still young, my lady. It is your heart I would like to capture." He looked so serious, he didn't know what atrocity he was committing with her heart. It was as if he had reached into her chest and was pressing her heart. Xandra had never had a man exert so much power over her. She wanted him to not only have her heart but she was ready to give him her life. And this was only the third date! When she didn't say anything more he looked over at her pensive look and asked "are you familiar with this road? I mean can you guess where we are going?" Xandra smiled, and looked out the window at the scenery, "yeah, I prefer to be surprised. I have been on this road to Hartebeespoort dam, it goes further through Pilanesberg National Park."

The sexual tension they both tried to conceal from each other was excruciating ever since they started the journey. There wasn't a lot of talking for two people who needed to get more acquainted yet behaved familiar with each other. Sean checked the GPS and slowed down, turning left he announced, "we are here at last." A strong wind blew by the time they parked the car in front of a huge building with a sign "Stephanie's on the Pier". It almost ripped the door from Sean's hand as he stepped out. The leaves on the ground and the terrace hissed as they flew luckily towards the opposite direction along with a cloud of dust. Sean closed his door and walked over to open Xandra's door, standing too close for her to move freely without rubbing against his chest. She looked up to his face acknowledging his help and he was smiling down at her, his eyes dancing with amusement. Xandra caught her breath *"this man has mastered the art of seduction, and I thought I knew how to flirt!"* she thought to herself. Nothing else mattered at this moment because it belonged to a man that deserved to be loved, and a woman that needed to be loved back. The only driving principles were the lust of the eyes, the lust of the flesh, and the pride of life. These clamored to be obeyed.

They were welcomed warmly by an elderly patron of the restaurant. She suggested a place for two on the terrace or the jetty but Sean declined both saying "I ordered a picnic basket for three under the name Cato." A male waiter exclaimed "Yes! Mr. Cato, your order is ready to go. Please follow me to check that all is in order and I shall carry it to the boat." Sean turned to Xandra, "would you like to look around and check out the curios in this place while I get this sorted?" She smiled adoringly at him, flirtatiously blinked her big eyes as nodded with understanding, and turned to walk away.

Sean had chartered a two-deck cruiser with a bar and lounge upstairs; dance floor, kitchen, and toilets downstairs. It was used for group cruise and fit to carry up to 50 people. They offered champagne welcome cocktails on arrival, a beautiful 2-hour scenic cruise with gourmet platters of oysters, baby octopus, tiger prawns, Mediterranean quinoa salad, tabbouleh, and a cheese platter, assorted bread, and tropical fruit. *"This is as romantic as it gets! No one had ever treated me like royalty."* She didn't think any man was capable of such finesse, and here was Sean being real; unpretentious, and not drooling over her either. He was calm and steady, dependable, and everything she ever dreamed of. *"I am nailed! This is textbook courting. This is how it should feel when you are right for each other. I want romance into old age."* She pondered.

At sunset, Sean announced, "It has been one of the best days of my life today, Xandra. I want more of this. Thanks for accepting to come out with me." Xandra smiled "thanks to you for surprising me this way. It has been wonderful Sean. I could get used to it." At that moment the music changed to "Everything" by Michael Buble. Sean got up from his seat and went down on one knee, pulling out a square blue box, he looked Xandra in the eyes and for about 6 seconds of deep penetrating scrutiny before asking "please Xandra be my wife. I have not known you too long, but find everything I want in you." Xandra was shocked that anyone would propose on the third date. Besides, he was still married to another woman. She was smitten by him but had a nagging feeling it wasn't right yet. She panicked and sat up straight not knowing what to say. "Please Sean dance with me." She pleaded. She couldn't say yes and she couldn't say no and hurt his feelings and lose him either. Sean stood up and extended his hand to her and drew her into an embrace for boat rocking dance that would decide their future. He held her close enough for her to feel his heart palpitations. She held her breath and let it out in gasps as they swayed to the music. Next on the playlist was Luther Vandross's Power of Love. Xandra quipped, "Yes. I will marry you, Sean." He reached for her chin with his right hand as he tightened his left around her waist. He lowered his face to hers and they kissed for a long time. The world around them ceased to exist. They were oblivious to time as daylight disappeared. The frogs croaked and crickets chirped but the lovers didn't hear it.

"So I strive always to keep my conscience clear before God and man." Acts 24:16 NIV

7

*"The point of living and of being an optimist is to be foolish enough
to believe the best is yet to come." --Peter Ustinov*

Sean was very convincing in his affections and quite sophisticated, a fairy tale romance ensued and Xandra was trapped. Despite all the affection, the flowers, chocolates and fine dining and dance dates, Xandra was scared because she was leaning towards the temptation to get involved with a man who was still married to another woman even if he claimed he was very unhappy and separated from her; and was hanging there for the sake of his children. She knew her faith, her upbringing, and conscious were against this union. Although Xandra knew deep inside her heart that this liaison was wrong, she felt justified every time she was introduced to more and more of his friends and family members. After all, so many people couldn't endorse the relationship with admiration and felicitation if it was morally wrong, or so she thought. Xandra's moral campus broke and was discarded. What does it take for the mighty to fall?

It still nagged Xandra from time to time that Sean was not only still legally married to another woman. The fact that he loved his children very much endeared him to her. When he confessed to Xandra that his marriage had failed, he had been unhappy living in strife and distrust. He confided that he had had extra-marital affairs and had also had children with other women because he was looking for love. She thought "this man needs to be loved and deserved to be happy". Xandra believed she would love him, satisfy his longing, and keep him happy because she had what it takes to do that. It was also obvious, to Xandra, that when a person confessed his past misdemeanors, it meant he regretted this behavior and had changed. It seemed he had found his balm and reason to change in Xandra, "his gift".

Every other day, he would come to her house for a short visit, and then announce that he had to go have high tea with his children because they depended on him to be happy. Of course, children need a stable parent who would love, protect, and reassure them in this time of strife. However, on such visits, he stayed out overnight. She justified this behavior even if it made her uneasy. She was haunted by her mother's instructions when she was sixteen. She was warned that "to get involved with a married man was a sin and a curse." Xandra resolved to never admit this error to her mother and resolve to defend her situation to others and even to herself.

Xandra resolved to love this man and wait for the situation to resolve, after all, she had prayed about it and asked God to sort it. She asked God if she could stay and get involved with this man and here she was with him, therefore, God must have blessed her. He was handsome, sophisticated, rich, generous, and a great lover. He was her fairytale prince. Everything she wanted in a man Sean had. Xandra felt loved, accepted, elevated, and almost fulfilled. But what was that lingering shame, nagging discontent that haunted her more often than she cared to admit to herself? This castle that Xandra was building seemed vulnerable. She raised a concrete wall around it by alienating herself from all those who tried to advise her; those who knew Sean very well, and the ones who professed to know how such men could not be trusted. She resolved not to confide her fears, insecurities, and shame. She could pray about it.

As was her habit on Saturday, Xandra woke up and got to the gym, then started her rounds of grooming – first the hair salon then window shopping. As she walked around she met an old friend who didn't look so well and she thought to herself *"could he be battling HIV? His skin and lips look like cases I have seen before. I better take a test before I get into bed with Sean. I'll propose it this evening over diner and if he refuses that shall be a sign to exit. If he accepts then he is safe and serious."*

Sean drove through her gate just as she parked her car at home. He walked over to the beaming Xandra. "Hey darling" he greeted. "Hello sweetie" she responded. They embraced and walked hand in hand to her front door. He took the keys from her hand and unlocked the door, ushering her into the open door with a hand on the small of her back. Sean was looking unhappy as he plopped into the sofa closest to the door. She noted this and waited, as she sat on the arm of the sofa. She didn't want to pry but badly wanted to know. "Sean darling, you look tired, may I offer you a glass of wine?" He responded with a sigh, "It is a little early for that but I could make us some tea." As he pattered around the kitchen, she moved to the bedroom and closed the windows, changed from her pumps into slippers, and put her handbag away before joining Sean in the living. She poured out some peanuts into a bowl and sat next to him on the two-seater sofa. "What is bothering you, my love?' Xandra asked looking at him sideways with a serious expression. "Nothing much. I went home early to see the children as they arrived from school and that woman started screaming and accusing me of having an affair, in the presence of the children." He rubbed his left palm across his brow and continued "I don't know how long I can put up with this. I need to move out because she is making all of us unhappy. She is verbally abusive, beats the children then runs to the kitchen crying, and starts to pray aloud!" Xandra kept silent. She felt sympathy while wondering why a grown man could bemoan that when he said he was separated from her. He continued "she has some friends who are ill-advising her. She meets them in church and then she spends hours watching evangelical channels on television – which the children and I can't stand. The woman used to be a professional cook but does not even produce a decent meal anymore. Dinner is always late." She put her cup of tea down and took his as well, frowning as she watched his distressed face. She asked "do you realize that she is fighting for her marriage? She wouldn't make a fuss if she didn't care. Maybe you should seek counseling and work it out." Xandra was surprised by that observation and this made her feel like an intruder. Again she had the nagging in her soul that she was tampering with someone's life. Sean sprang quickly to his defense "she doesn't listen and I can't stand that. I do not believe in having a counselor tell two people how to feel and what to do." "But it would help your cause to hear each other out and give your marriage a chance. If she is praying a lot, she must be distressed. If she isn't cooking like she used to she might be depressed and disillusioned." Xandra spoke out in wisdom, genuinely putting herself in another woman's shoes. "Just let it go, I shall figure it out. I am happy to be here with you. I would like to take a nap before my next meeting tonight. I am meeting a bank manager about funding for my oil pipeline tender. Would you join us?" He said, deflecting from the gloom of the subject. Xandra had heard enough that she needed to process. Besides she needed to travel very early in the morning, out of town, for a meeting with project implementing partners. "No thanks. I need to sleep early for a meeting tomorrow. Come on lie down on my bed and rest. I am going to read through my documents in preparation." She held him by the hand and took him to the bedroom. She mumbled an excuse, as he undressed to lie down. She did not get into bed but walked back to the living room to wallow in her thoughts and deal with her conscience.

Two hours later, Sean walked into the living room looking fresh and more cheerful. He walked to her and kissed her. "I waited for a cuddle and you disappeared." He accused. Xandra saw this as an opportunity to propose HIV/AIDS testing. "Sean, I think we are moving pretty fast in this relationship and as a matter of principle, we must have HIV/AIDS tests done before we get into the sack. We both ..." She tried to explain but he put a finger to her lips and with a sweet smile said "why one test? Why not have a full health check. I know the perfect place and shall make an appointment for us." Xandra was blown away. *This man is ready! He is serious and worth trusting.* Sean kissed her passionately and left her happier.

"The beginning of wisdom is this: Get wisdom. Though it cost all you have, get understanding." - Proverbs 4:7 NIV

8

Come live with me and be my love,
And we will all the pleasures prove,
That Valleys, groves, hills, and fields,
Woods, or steepy mountain yields.
By Christopher Marlowe

Three days later, Sean obtained an appointment for and executive health check to which she took Xandra. The fasted and went early morning to the hospital executive lounge. After the specimens were taken, the lovers were treated to an English breakfast. The test results would be ready on the fourth day. That same day at noon, Sean chartered a helicopter to his hometown of Roodeplaat so they could get there quickly and back for his business meetings in the evening. Sean took Xandra to meet his parents and had one visit to his eldest sister where he announced, "I have found the wife I have been looking for." The parents admired Xandra. If she ever had a doubt, Sean's actions and words convinced her of his sincere intentions, and the deal was sealed. She had been greatly honored.

The weekend ended fast and the whole week passed in a haze. Mid-week, Sean picked Xandra from her workplace at 16:00 surprising her, for an early diner. This is the first time for him to come to her workplace. He did not get out of the car but waited, parked next to hers. The navy-blue Mercedes tore through the countryside at 120km, fast enough for a highway but too fast to enjoy the scenery. There was an air of urgency about this trip. They drove one hour out of town to a country club. Sean had up picked the test results from the clinic and their curiosity was part of the vibe. They ordered Campari and orange for an aperitif and sat in the lounge poring over the medical reports, as their table was getting set in front of a fireplace. It was a chilly day and perfect for snuggling up. The first thing Xandra scanned for was HIV/AIDS test and it was negative for both. She was in excellent health, and she knew it. Sean tests were great too except for high cholesterol which he attributed to regular rare steak. This was not worrying at all. Dinner was filled with a comfortable easy conversation about political scandals and the people Sean had met recently. He told Xandra "my friend Santino swindled me on a deal. I have lost a lot of money and have employed some lawyers to collect." She listened intently at his business talk, intrigue but also wondering *"we are from quite different worlds. How are we going to relate? Never mind, I know how to switch my mind off when I get bored and make sounds to encourage him."* He smiled and stopped himself "Xandra, you are a particularly good listener. I don't want to bore you with my stories. I have more news. I contacted an agent to get us a bigger house than your cottage because I love entertaining." Xandra was surprised because they had not discussed the need for a bigger place and timing for living together. She smiled despite her thoughts and agreed "I love entertaining". She didn't say it aloud, but she was thinking of *"and more rooms when we start a family"*.

The following day, when the disconcertingly gorgeous Sean turned up on Xandra's front door carrying bags of his clothes, followed by workmen coming to install cable TV she felt flattered. Could she doubt a man who has put his words into action and made the bold move to move in with her? Could she push the subject of his marital status at this stage?

He waltzed into the house, kissed her, and dropped his bags onto the sofa, and pulled her to the bedroom after giving the workmen instructions to go ahead with the connections. Xandra loved having a man in control. The stage for cohabiting was set.

9

"Even as the archer loves the arrow that flies, so too he loves the bow that remains constant in his hands" – Nigerian Proverb

It was now two months since Sean and Xandra met, and a week after he moved in with her. It was time for a family reunion of Xandra's family. Relatives from all over the country and those living abroad returned to congregate at her grandfather's house for a two days' party. As they got into bed, Xandra turned to Sean, "darling, I am expected home for an annual family reunion next week. Would you like to come and meet my parents?". "You cannot go next week, I made plans for us to travel to Tanzania to visit the Ngorongoro crater. We would fly to Nairobi, Kenya, and drive through the Maasai Mara, on to the Tanzania border through Massai land, through Arusha to the famous Ngorongoro crater. Besides, it is my birthday next weekend," he announced with authority. "Oh no! we can do that when we get back, besides my mother is big on birthdays and you will be celebrated by a multitude. You will love my family because they are an affectionate and funny lot. It is a ceremony that you must never miss. I shall then have to ask for extended leave to take the trip you have organized," stated Xandra victoriously. She reached over and switched off the light and then put her phone into silence mode. Sean lay back on his pillow with both arms cradling his head and fell silent for a while pondering this counterproposal. Xandra moved closer and put her left arm around his chest and nuzzled closer to him. He turned around and drew her into his arms and said with sweet finality, "I would love to meet your family. Let me schedule my meetings and ask my secretary to make a flight, hotel, and vehicle bookings." Xandra kissed him passionately, saying to herself "I shall give him everything he asks of me."

The calls from an irate wife never ceased, day and night. Xandra overheard the shrill questioning "who is that woman you have taken up with? Why can't she wait for us to part properly before she interferes." His calm responses to her were always along the lines of "calm down and stop these lies you are listening to. Take care of the children beware of those friends who are misleading you. I shall talk to you when I get home." Each time Sean was done with these calls he would exude self-pity and long-suffering with words like "she is going crazy and listening to her friends and lies. I need to go and check on the well-being of my children soon." Xandra was uneasy and she knew trouble was brewing but she was not willing to dwell on it or face the truth. Since she wasn't consulting with anyone she could only pray and rely on her understanding.

Sean started leaving to visit his children and staying away for up to three days and nights at a time. He would pass by the cottage to check on Xandra and cry on her shoulder about his and the children's sad predicament. "Sorry darling, let me sort the children and find a way out," he said. Xandra was determined to be supportive and even though she didn't like the situation, she resolved to be patient.

The week passed fast and it was Thursday, morning, Xandra was set to travel on Thursday night to be with her family for the entire weekend. Although Sean was scheduled to travel with her, she conditioned herself for any eventualities since he didn't talk about the travel anymore. When Xandra arrived home from the gym at 19:00, Sean had arrived and was fixing diner, with a bottle of red wine open. She was excited to see him and even more excited to see a suitcase in the corner and six large, wrapped gifts next to it. Sean's eyes followed hers as he asked "I thought you were too busy to go shopping and I asked my secretary to pick up some gifts for your parents and others. I hope you don't mind. Have you packed?" Xandra exclaimed "yes! And yes! What would I do without you? Thanks, Sean." She walked over to him by the stove and kissed him passionately. *"This is going to be a blast!"* she thought to herself, all doubts and uneasiness of the past week gone. "That smells delicious, what is it?" she asked. "It is paella. I hope you love mussels." "Mhh I don't particularly fancy them and won't eat escargot ever! I won't kiss you if you eat them." She pouted and turned towards the gifts. "So what is in these big packages?" Sean pretended not to hear the question and walked to the drawer to get the cutlery, leaving her to press for a response. Xandra wasn't to be put off. She walked to the dining table and set a place for two, poured two wine glasses, and joined Sean by the stove. "Are you going to tell me what presents you have bought for who or will you leave me to guess?" This elicited a laugh from Sean who kissed her on the forehead and told her she was going to have to be patient and be surprised too. *"How lucky can I be? This man is so different!"* she thought. Although Xandra wanted to hear more about the situation with the children and what the future had in store, she restrained her curiosity because she thought better than to push a man out or into a decision. She chose not to tell him how sad and confused she felt every time he was gone overnight.

"The fact is, you have had five husbands, and the man you now have is not
your husband. What you have just said is quite true." John 4:18 NIV

10

"Listen, my son, to your father's instruction and do not forsake your mother's teaching." Proverbs 1:8 NIV

At sunrise on Friday, the plane touched down at King Mswati III International Airport and the air was cold and invigorating. As Sean and Xandra walked out of the airport, they were met by a driver with a placard inscribed "Mr. Cato". The waiting driver took them to their hotel and handed the vehicle papers and keys to Sean. The two love birds checked into their room and ordered room service. After breakfast, Sean made some calls as Xandra watched the news on TV. They had five hours before they were expected at her home where they would visit with family before going to her grandfather's house in the evening. Her parents had been told they were going to meet her fiancée. Although the tradition would have required a formal asking of her hand before engagement, they opted to let it go because Xandra had already been given away to her first husband and the clan would have to agree to the new extenuating circumstances.

On arrival, the entire Rafiq family was outside waiting for their arrival. As Sean stepped out of the car, he was grabbed into an embrace by Xandra's eldest brother, Sadiq. The passed on to another family member, and another until he was face to face with a tall, stately elderly man with kind smiling eyes. He guessed this must be Mr. Rafiq and extended his hand for a greeting. The grip of Mr. Rafiq's handshake was firm, dry, and warm. The excitement around was dizzying because there were ululations from the women and children. He noticed briefly as a beautiful girl, who could have been mistaken for Xandra hugged her sister tight. He calmly turned around at a melodic sound announcing "welcome home Sean. We are happy to meet you, at last, we have heard a lot about you." It was unmistakably, Xandra's mother. He extended his arm for a handshake but was pulled into an embrace. This love and acceptance on arrival are more than he expected. Another young man received him into a hug, introducing himself as Mica, Xandra's younger brother. Next, it was Xandra's lookalike opening her arms to hug him and introducing herself as Ruby. It was an epic homecoming. Sean was still nervous but happy to have witnessed this because it gave him a glimpse of his wife to be. They were ushered into the house and straight to a table that was sitting about twenty people with several dishes of assorted African, Arab, and Continental dishes. *I wonder what the main banquet will look like if this is family lunch,* he thought.

When Mr. Rafiq sat down and folded his hands to call for prayer, everyone instantly went silent, and they all proceeded to make the sign of the cross as he led the grace, "Bless us, O Lord, and these, Thy gifts, which we are about to receive from Thy bounty. Through Christ, our Lord. Amen." And everyone chorused "Amen" after which the noise consisting of cutlery, clanking plates, greetings, questions, comments started. Sean was seated to the immediate right of Mr. Rafiq near the head of the table while Xandra sat next to her mother to the left of Mr. Rafiq. These were seats of honor. Everyone seemed to have a different kind of drink before them. Mica asked Rafiq "will you have water, wine, beer, or buganu (marula beer). "I shall have buganu please" announced Sean to the surprise and pleasure of all. Lunch was a two-hour affair filled with jokes and much camaraderie. As soon as Mr. Rafiq got up it was time to leave the lunch table and all the men followed him outside to sit under a tree to chat and more drinks were served. "This buganu is a very good brew" complimented Sean looking over at Mica who grinned and brought forth a jug to pour him some more. Sean did not decline. "Mica thank you for getting me drank on my first visit" he joked. Sadiq warned "there is a price for that Sean. Mica doesn't do anything for free" and everyone laughed as Mica protested. The women were cleaning up and when they all came out, they were carrying pots and baskets ready to go to the first evening of the family banquet. Mr. and Mrs. Rafiq both came to Sean's side and told him "we expect you back tomorrow for breakfast and lunch. We want to hear more about you and your people and your intentions for our Xandra." Sean nodded with a slight bow of respect with a right hand to his chest he responded "all good. Thank you for receiving me. I look forward to seeing more of you." *I wonder if I have to answer questions about myself at the banquet,"* he thought nervously.

On arrival, there was hardly any parking space left and although the compound looked like a football field every inch was covered with children and adults. "One can hardly believe a woman could have so many relatives. Are these all your relatives or just neighbors and friends?" Exclaimed Sean. Xandra proudly confirmed "all of the blood relatives my love. Friends and neighbors join us only on Sunday. I am glad you came, Sean. You will be scrutinized and interrogated for sure, be warned." The evening passed as expected with men sitting outside, and women congregating inside. Xandra came looking for Sean to depart to the hotel at midnight. They were all exhausted.

Saturday morning came too soon!

11

"A person's character is like pregnancy it cannot be hidden."

~African Proverb

A call came through on Sean's number and there was a shrill woman on the other end when he answered. He sat up in bed "What is this about?" he asked her. Xandra pretended not to hear but couldn't help listening in to solve the nagging questions that she dared not confront. She heard "Who is that woman that is taking you away from your family? Where are you anyway? …" This woman talked with the authority of a woman exercising her rights. *I bet it is his wife and the relationship was solid. I am pathetic, illegitimate, and interference to his life.* Xandra felt embarrassment at hearing that but sorry for Sean at the same time, and got out of bed. Not before she heard him say "I told you I am away working, we shall talk about this when I get back." He concluded and hang up.

Despite that outburst, Xandra still respected and believed Sean's intentions and noble standing. However, she did not want to make him uncomfortable with her inquiries and too proud to sound pathetic she kept silent. Jumped into the shower. Sean walked into the bathroom and went about brushing his teeth as if nothing had happened. He then proceeded to join her in the shower; grabbed the shower gel and started to lather her back from the nape. Xandra was flattered and distracted.

At breakfast, Mica joined them to say they were expected home early. Sean excused himself to make a call as the siblings continued chatting. He talked long after breakfast had been cleared and looked purposeful as he passed around the terrace pool a distance from them. Mica asked "when are you planning to get married big sis? It is about time you started a family, you know" he added as he pointed to the watch on his arm." Xandra smiled affectionately "we haven't talked about that yet. Don't worry, I shall have the dozen in pairs to make up for the lost time." Sean walked over and suggested they leave to be home in time because "I need to make an impression on my father and mother, or it might cost me greatly!" he teased.

One cannot confront what they won't admit is wrong. It is easier to push it under the rug and focus on the positives in the hope that the wrongs will right themselves. *"That woman wants her man back. She has a hold on him and he won't give reconciliation a chance while he is taking up with me."* Xandra thought. *But she* was determined to have fun today.

12

Love the truth even if it hurts you,
Hate lies even if they help you.

~African Proverb~

The party had been a blast and the two lovers were exhausted. Sean had impressed the family with his suave ways, thoughtfulness, and knowledge. He even assured Xandra's parents that he had good intentions for their daughter which he intended to make clear as soonest possible. They neglected to say that they lived together.

Just before leaving the family home for the party, Xandra's mother pulled her aside and confided "this man is very handsome my child. I want you to check his life carefully because a man at the age of forty-three years should have a legitimate reason to be separating from his wife of twenty-three years. If he loves children as he says, is he going to leave them? Married men seldom leave their wives for hotter, younger ones." She paused awhile, searching for her daughter's face. "Do not get involved with a married man my child. God will not endorse Adultery. Before you decide to commit to him and bring him for a formal wedding, I shall need to see a divorce certificate. I do not want you to get hurt Xandra. We all love Sean already, but take your time and study him." Xandra was obliged to respond. She wanted to confide her fears to her mother but all she could say was "I have heard Sean's exchange with his wife, and he has confirmed to me that the relationship is over, and he intends to divorce her. His friends and family have all confirmed to me that I have made him very happy because his wife was making him miserable." Xandra stood up as her mother remained seated "Then why is he still in her bed if he is divorcing her? Where does he sleep while visiting his children? Don't you know that a man must prove he is separated from his before he files for divorce?". Xandra shrugged and almost pleaded "mama, I am afraid to stress him out already, but promise to be careful." She desperately wanted to run out of that room and hide her face because she knew her mother was right.

All-day Sean looked happy and attentive to his in-laws. A few times he poured drinks to refill the men's drinks. He cracked some jokes and looked like he was one of them. He charmed them all greatly. On the drive to the hotel, he turned to quiet Xandra asked "are you alright my love? What is on your mind?" She smiled broadly and pretended to be tired "I had a great time. I am so happy that it scares me sometimes how lucky I am to be here with you." He reached out and held her hand and drew it to his leg, caressing her fingers gently. "Everything will be alright; you have nothing to be afraid of."

That night, Xandra boldly told Sean "I am running out of contraceptives and might not be safe anymore." He assuredly smiled and pulled her into an embrace "Children are a gift from God. I always wanted one but now I know better. We shall have a beautiful one." Xandra confided "I always wanted six children but after having enough savings and investment. Are you sure you are ready for this?" He said it again "Children are a gift from God Xandra." And that sealed it because God was mentioned. If God was in the equation, that endorsed it.

By the time Xandra woke up, Sean was sitting up reading messages. She moved closer to him and lay on his chest. "Tomorrow by this time I shall be in the office, and all this will be history. Thank you for taking the time to come home with me. It was fun having you here and my family adores you." He pulled her closer and said matter-of-factly "My woman cannot work. If she has to work, it is with the family business." Xandra exclaimed "I believe a woman should earn and support her family. I have obligations even here at home. I am the one who maintains my parents. Did I tell you that I have some property that needs to be developed?" Sean looked over her and pulled her chin up "I can take good care of you. I shall give you an allowance monthly from which you can support your family and do whatever you want. But in the family, we have to pull our resources together so that what is mine is yours and what is yours is mine." Xandra protested, "I know that you have to maintain your wife and the children so I suggest that whatever wealth you have made belongs to them and I shall have nothing to do with it. In the same vein, whatever property I have invested in belongs to me for the maintenance of my family because my parents cannot become your dependents. Besides, that will be the inheritance that I leave to our children." Sean didn't dispute that but had a counteroffer. "I shall check with my business partners to buy me out of a venture so that I can set you up with a laundry business I have had my eye on. My friends and I had planned to buy it for our wives to partner and run it but my wife refused so we shelved the idea. You can earn a salary and, in that way, you are employed in the family business with flexible hours. I shall introduce you to the current owner so they can train you when you finish your contract. That way you will keep busy." Xandra couldn't argue with that solid plan. "*This is a sure way forward and her career change was sorted. Now I shall have both a new career and family with a man who loves to take care of his wife and children – kind of rare quality in men these days. God, you love me and have blessed me at last.*"

As if this was a fine moment to press forward the rules of engagement, Sean sat up and announced "I also have a curfew for my wife. She must not drive around at night. She must be home by six o'clock and can entertain friends and family at home." Xandra thought it reasonable because after all, she didn't need to go anywhere. "She smiled and waited for more. "You need to learn my culture too because women are taken to a man's family and must fit in and not the other way round," he said. "Any more I should know about? She quipped teasingly. Sean responded, "now go hit the shower so I can feed you". Xandra felt spoiled and thought to herself "*if he asks me for life, I shall give it to him.*" It felt exhilarating to have a man in power, and for an advocate of gender equality it was also contradictory. Xandra trusted in her wit and garb to manage every situation. Sean would be loved, honored, and served. She was going to serve him even if he trampled her. God knows what veil fell over her face but at this moment, she didn't only decide to give her life to but her soul as well to Sean. In just a few words, the relationship transformed into master and servant, superior, and subordinate. Xandra resented the control of men and had sworn again abuse in any form. She despised the fear and control her father had over her mother and had sworn to never allow such a relationship. She did not see any similarity in the demands made of her.

Something in the atmosphere had changed and now Xandra felt a step lower than Sean. He had the upper hand and she felt vulnerable and in need of his approval. Sean did not change much but his tone of authority and hand on the small of her back screamed ownership. When landed at Johannesburg, Sean had two drivers waiting for them and it was only then that he told her that he needed to attend to something at the office and they would meet at home. He gave orders "Kubal, get my wife home safely and park the car at the office." "Yes sir! Welcome back," Kubal responded grinning.

13

"I am a great and sublime fool. But then I am God's fool, and all His works must be contemplated with respect." -Mark Twain

Xandra waited by the terrace for hours on end until midnight. She woke up on the couch at dawn and checked her phone for a message. Sean did not come home. He neither called nor sent a message. She felt pain her hurt. *"Maybe he worked until morning. Or could he be at the other home with the children?"* She felt disrespected that he did not let her know he wasn't coming home and did not call her. She tried to call him then stopped herself as the thought *"he might be irritated if he is at the other home, and I get him into trouble. … what if he is in trouble, injured or robbed?"* After what seemed like half an hour, Xandra sent a message to Sean "are you alright? Please let me know if you are safe. She waited a while and a message came *"I am sorry darling, I got so tired I forgot to call you. I worked late and came to see the children then fell asleep. I shall see you shortly after my first meeting."* She was happy he was alive and well, but an indescribable feeling came over her to realize that the situation was complicated, and she was in it. It was not jealousy. It was not confusing. It was discontent that put a knife in her heart because deep inside she wanted like to run away, fast, and far away. She could not run away from the man who loved and needed her. She did not want to dwell on this matter, so she jumped into the shower and went to work. It helped to keep busy.

When Xandra got home, she smelt Sean's cologne as soon as the door opened. She knew he had been home and that was consoling, although he did not call her the whole day. His shirt was on the bed and although it was not dirty, it smelt strongly of a mix of sweat and cologne and she loved it! She grabbed the shirt and held it to her nose, inhaling deeply. She lay down with the shirt close to her face, smelling Sean. *"Even his sweat smells so good,"* she thought. She fell asleep and woke up two hours later. It was dark and her windows were still open. She put the shirt into the laundry basket and took a shower. She did not want to cook so she made popcorn and poured a glass of wine. She had skipped the gym, anxious to get home to Sean for an explanation. It was now ten o'clock and he had neither come back nor called. She restrained from calling him, out of fear of being a pest to him, getting disappointed, and to safeguard personal pride.

"I am supposed to feel happy right now, but I am not. It is a new relationship and I want to run away fastest before it crumbles. It is too early for him to be bored with me. Besides, no man takes a woman to meet his parents if he is playing with her. He must be in a bind and needs my support". Xandra reasoned with herself. She went to bed hoping Sean would come home. She chose not to have any expectations, but she listened to every sound out there – the dogs running past her window, cars driving past, coughing of the gate watchman.

Xandra woke up to the sound of jingling keys and the front door locking. She had the urge to jump out of bed to attend to him but chose to pretend to be asleep. She looked at the bedside clock and it indicated four o'clock. As he entered the bedroom she turned around, raised her head to look at him with sleepy eyes, and smiled at him, then put her head down and turned the other way. "Sorry to wake you up darling," Sean said at the same time hanging his blazer onto the seat next to the bed. He sat on the bed and removed his shoes slowly, sighed but said nothing more. He then removed the socks and yawned getting up to go to the bathroom. He came back to bed, quietly inching closer to her, and drew her into an embrace. No words were said, no expected excuses given.

Xandra woke up wanting an explanation but hurriedly showered, dressed up, picked her gym bag, and handbag leaving the house without hesitation. She knew she had to do something but she didn't know what, so she did what always works for her, go to exercise, then to work. She needed to find an explanation within herself because she knew this situation was not ideal and sensed something was not right. Just as she got into the office, her mobile phone rang, she checked and it was Sean "hey, you are wake!" is all she could say. "Good morning darling. Why didn't you wake me up? Can you meet me for breakfast at Café Rouge?" Sean invited. "I have a staff meeting every Tuesday morning until noon, maybe we can meet over lunch." Xandra was filled with mixed emotions of happiness and an element of loss at the same time. She wanted to be with Sean but was duty-bound to go to the meeting. She wanted an explanation for Sean's behavior and assurance this was not going to be the norm. "I shall send my driver to pick up at twelve then because I shall be in a meeting, "Sean told her. "Alright. I love you." She offered and "I love you too darling," he responded with a laugh.

As Xandra put the phone down she felt excitement and shame because they were still keeping their relationship a secret from her workplace and many people. She wasn't confident to claim a man that was still married. She felt like an impostor wife. The human conscience is an amazing creation. One cannot shut it out or manipulate it.

14

Do not throw away the oars before you reach the shore. — African Proverb

Xandra woke up and looked across at Sean who was still deeply asleep. He had arrived shortly after midnight. It seems as if the lunch was to appease and not only make her aware that he would come home late again. Before they went to visit her parents, he had taken her to several of his meetings and she believed he was out working. But this was not a normal life for one to work through the day and the night. He did not give her a reasonable explanation over lunch for the day before but only to say "I am sorry I have to work late often because many people I would like to meet are attentive after work. All deals are sealed at diner and drinks in the evening." How could Xandra dispute that, seeing he was a prosperous and generous man?

As she started to get out of bed, Sean reached over and pulled her close. She couldn't resist the warm embrace even though she just wanted to get to her knees and pray then run to the gym and to work. Something about routines and the familiar help one to keep the façade of normal. "Stay with me this morning my wife," he invited. "I can't. I have to go to work, my contract has only three more months and I need to get a good performance evaluation from my boss." She explained. "But my wife shouldn't have to work for any boss. I am going to see the children for high tea today and shall be back to pick you up for diner with my brother." Even as Sean talked, Xandra felt nausea welling up inside and she wriggled free to run to the bathroom. She got to the toilet in time to throw up. This is unusual, she thought. Sean came up to her and held her by the waist asking "what is it, my love? You are having morning sickness?" and firmly stated, "you are pregnant!" Xandra felt confused because she didn't have a hangover, no stomachache, or an indication of food poisoning. She contemplated Sean's statement and remembered the incident with his shirt. Shock hit her as she looked up at Sean "I know when my woman is pregnant," he said. "I have to go to work but shall get a tester from the pharmacy on the way out," she stated.

By the time Xandra dressed up, Sean arrived back with a tester, from the pharmacy half a mile from their cottage. He made her a cup of tea and asked her to test before she went to work. Xandra felt jitters at the changes in her life. After drinking tea, she had a bowl of muesli and ate an orange. She didn't feel nausea anymore. She was biding her time. She called her secretary to say that she would be one hour late because she was going to a meeting on her way. A lie she hated but was comfortable to make up. She then went to the bathroom to have the test done as Sean waited in the bedroom. He seemed excited and that assured her. She walked into the room and gave the tester to Sean, "you are right! I am pregnant." Sean "picked her up and hugged her tight. We are going to have a baby that is as beautiful as the mother," he exclaimed. Xandra had not expected this much excitement from a man who already had children and she felt very loved. "I know it will be a boy. My mother had two boys before she got a girl," she declared. "Oh, you don't determine that. In my family we start with girls; you will see." They parted for the day.

On her way out, Sean asked Xandra to "please tell your maid not to wash my clothes. I dry clean all of them. She also shouldn't use too much polish on my shoes. Can you teach her? I shall teach you how to fold my shirts and hang my coats and pants. You don't treat suits the same as jeans." He said pursing his mouth intending criticism in jest. "Alright, you can teach me all that. I never had to fuss over a man's laundry before. See you later." Xandra felt happy that he was going to teach her and that she was learning something from him. She wondered, though, why he wouldn't talk to the maid himself and decided it she would suggest it to him. Even for the gender equality activist, the net tightens as she is knowingly subdued by dominance in a romantic glove.

Diner with Donald, Sean's brother was quiet. The brothers talked formally as if they were strangers. This was strange for Xandra whose family was very and warm. Donald seemed reverent towards his brother and very uncomfortable. When Sean left the table to take a call, Xandra engaged Donald into a conversation and brightened up and seemed comfortable until Sean returned to the table. There was an obvious difference in social class and the relationship didn't seem equal. Sean seemed condescending while talking to Donald in their ethnic language. He had the money and power over his brother who seemed to need something from him. It was not a pleasant meeting after all. On the way home, Xandra asked Sean why Donald seemed so reverent and uncomfortable. Sean signed and explained "we used to fight a lot while we were young. Donald is my mom's favorite and as much as I have helped him out in business, he continues to cheat and undermine me. This is the first time we are meeting in one year." That was a very sad confession. Sean continued in a resigned tone "my family is very clique and difficult. You have to stay away from them. I won't encourage them to come home either." Sean sounded determined and Xandra let it go although she planned to change them all and teach them how family loves each other.

When they got home, Sean seemed irritable as he found his shoes in the spot where he left them, unpolished. He called to Xandra, "when are you going to teach your maid to clean my shoes?" Xandra rounded the corner upset but trying to remain calm and defended herself "I was out all day and she was gone when I came home. I shall polish them for you and leave her a note in the morning." "Please do because when I get frustrated, I become abusive," warned Sean as he walked past Xandra to the bedroom. Xandra thought to herself "how does anyone abuse me? It can't happen and I know Sean doesn't mean it the way he said it." She pushed the thought out of her mind and proceeded to get ready for bed. *Marriage means taking care of your man so he never requires anything. A woman takes care of his clothes, food, and clean house. I remember 70 years old Kagu telling us that a wife must be a maid, a nurse, and sexually uninhibited like a prostitute to her husband. I gotta work on that.* Xandra went to sleep determined to be indispensable. Sean still partly belonged to her but she was going to take on the wife role pending holy matrimony.

15

For lack of discipline they will die, led astray by their own great folly. – Proverbs 5:23 NIV

The following morning, Sean told Xandra that he was scheduled to meet bankers early in the morning because he had lost a lot of money in a venture. He was planning to get rid of some of his cars to keep up with bank repayments and pump money into his farm. She listened carefully and wanted so much to help. She suggested, "let us put the renting of a bigger house on hold and put the curtain and furniture orders on hold until you have recovered." Sean protested "no that will continue. No need to delay although I cannot pay for the curtains now because I have to pay school fees." Xandra stepped in with another suggestion "alright then I shall withdraw the money schedule to complete payment on the house I bought and pay for the curtains for now." Sean did not protest or thank her but grabbed his coat with a sigh, turned around, and kissed her on the forehead "Don't worry about anything. You must have a great day and take it, easy darling. We shall sort this out soon." Xandra couldn't wait to go pay for the curtains because it would ease the burden on Sean and give her ownership as well.

Her phone rang as she started the car and it was Sean "darling, I shall be home early for diner tonight. We need to start having home-made meals. You need to start eating healthy." Xandra was flattered and meekly responded "of course darling." The anxiety hit her because she was not confident to cook for a man who ate in restaurants so regularly. She had not cooked for anyone in over two years but trusted in her creative abilities. *I have to get home early. Maybe I can go to the market at lunch so that I could go to the gym after work,* she thought. The day went by so fast, and she was too busy to go to the market at lunch. She opted to order salad and quiche to take home for dinner and would buy food on the way home, to cook the following day. When she went to pick the order, she found the butcher next to a Russian restaurant, so she bought a T-bone steak because Sean loved it.

When Sean arrived, the table was set, and food was in the oven keeping warm. He opted to shower and change before diner. Xandra wanted to serve the food hot, therefore she pan-fried the steak, well done, and put it in foil, and placed it in the oven. She opened a bottle of Cabernet Sauvignon and placed it on the table. Sean walked into the dining look suave in a navy-blue tracksuit and barefooted. She caught her breath and turned away to dutifully serve her husband. He went straight to the table and poured out two glasses of wine as Xandra placed the food on the table dish after dish. The sat down and Sean insisted she leads the grace, which she did. She then hastily uncovered the quiche, unwrapped the baguette, the T-bone steaks, and Mash potato. She turned to pour dressing over the vinaigrette dressing over salad and heard a sigh. When she looked at Sean, her heart sank. He looked dissatisfied as he commented "you overcooked the steak. I like mine rare and juicy. Are we going to have some gravy with this food?" The fall from elation to shame is high and swift. "I am sorry darling all meals must have gravy, or we will choke, and I don't eat sandwiches," he added. That meal did not go well. The wine was not rejected. Sean served himself salad and baguette. He noted the silence and tried to make an ugly situation light by announcing that he would bring his professional cook as soon as they move house. Xandra was crushed. She did not enjoy the quiche, salad, and baguette that she normally loved. She would never see steak the same way again.

When they moved to the living room to watch the news, Sean put an arm around Xandra's shoulders and announced, "I am leaving a woman who gave me eighty percent and expect one hundred percent, not twenty." He had raised the bar and set the standard. The noose tightened. She was pregnant and playing wife. Xandra knew that she had conquered much in her career and would ace this challenge. Sean offered her a shot of brandy and she accepted. She was aware that pregnant women are not allowed to drink but she had seen many in her family do that, so she justified that it made babies smart and was harmless. She was not going to stop, and Sean was alright with it.

They loved Friday nights because they could sit and chat through the night and wake up late. He was never in a hurry to wake up early or leave home on Saturday until the evening. The talked about a lot of things and she heard of his past conquests.

He told her that he had fallen in love and got married at the age of twenty-two years and his wife was older than him by five years. She was perfect and he was jealous of her. However, he confessed that he was young and wild and cheated on her a lot including having children with the women. He had three children he had refused to admit to her. He had no remorse but talked like a man confessing his past. Xandra was not alarmed but flattered that he loved her enough to come clean of his past weaknesses, which meant he had changed. He justified his behavior "I was unhappy because my wife was quarrelsome. I had a lot of money and just stayed away," he said. When she asked him if he realized that he hurt his wife, he defended himself with "she drove me to it." Xandra had obtained information to save her later, so she neither nagged nor constrained him, and did not starve him of sex determined to keep him happy. Or so she thought. Camillo di Cavour once said "I have discovered the art of deceiving diplomats. I tell them the truth and they never believe me." Xandra was not deceived but she deceived through her desire to build something special with Sean. All wisdom of her father went down the drain. She wasn't going to relate this to anyone because she knew they would see right through the deception and tell her something she didn't want to hear. She listened to Sean's stories attentively without exclamation, a show of surprise or judging. He complimented her on being a good listener and they drank some more wine.

In the morning, Xandra woke up early and went for a jog in shorts and a sweatshirt. When she got back, Sean was waiting at the terrace and looked unhappy. She walked into the house and went straight to join him, but he steered her into the house and told her "my wife cannot run on the road, and certainly not dressed in shorts. The men will look at you and get ideas. It is as good as letting them touch you." Xandra protested "but this is what I have worn always, and it isn't skimpy or indecent. Besides no man even looked at me or made advances. The road is safe Sean, and you should join me." "No way! I don't even want your instructors in the gym to come to help you to stretch because they are touching my woman. I shall build you a gym at home." She was flattered that he loved to protect her but couldn't get around not wearing shorts. She grimaced at the thought and Sean saw that. "Darling, why did you make that face? I don't like people making faces." She raised her brows in surprise, and he exclaimed "yeah that face is disrespectful." Xandra laughed with surprise "that is my shocked, surprised facial expression. It is not disrespectful my love." The more she talked the more her face contorted with expressions and Sean could not bear it! *"Oh, my goodness! Am I to not express myself at all? That is easy. I shall try to be expressionless,"* she resolved silently but said, "I am sorry darling, I did not mean to offend you." She thought it best to go shower and brood over these things in private.

When she came out of the bedroom, Sean had made tea, cut oranges, and was not chopping vegetables to make omelets. She set the table and positioned the bead in the toaster, then drank a glass of water. She drank a glass of water to keep her distracted. Sean continued his lessons on what he liked and how. He liked his meals hot, and the eggs had to be served straight from the pan to the plate. His tea had to be made to a certain standard – measure the rations and keep it simmering for best results. At least he was giving her tips and for that, she was grateful although it reminded her how inadequate she was. Until today, she thought his sun rose and set in her. She knew now he was in charge, and she was an apprentice of whom much was expected. She had read a quote from Robert South that *"all deception in the course of life is indeed nothing else but a lie reduced to practice, and falsehood passing from words into things."*

When they woke up from an afternoon nap, Xandra proceeded to prepare high tea. She got a call from an old friend; she knew from high school days visiting from London. He invited her and some other friends for a night out on the town. She said that she would revert to him. When she carried the tea tray to the terrace, she found Sean hanging up as he said "see you in an hour to the person on the other end. She beamed at him and asked if he had plans to go out. "I have been looking for an investor who has now come into town and my friend Martin has secured a meeting for us this evening". "Oh alright, I also would like to go to Sandton square to meet with an old school friend. I knew him from high school and our offices were next to each other," Xandra relayed. "You are just mentioning it now? And you are going to meet a man? Women do not have male friends and especially married women. You need to talk to your mother. My woman cannot go out to meet a man in the night." He declared angrily. Xandra was petrified, angry, and defiant at the same time. It would take some getting used to give lose that ground. Xandra stood still as she listened to a tirade that she didn't believe in. She so badly wanted to grimace but was not allowed to make facial expressions. He concluded with "Second marriages are never successful just as beautiful women are not to be married." What that cruel retort he ignored the tea, rose, and left the house. Xandra did not go out. She had a night of much thought. *"I have to get someone to talk to."*

Marriage was proving very complicated. She would figure it out for the sake of her unborn child and make her dream come true.

16

"Pay attention to yourselves! If your brother or sister sins against you, rebuke them; and if he repents, forgive them," – Luke 17:3 NIV

Sean did not return that night. He did not call or send a text message either. It hurt so bad and scared her that he had started to disrespect her. The more she gave in to his demands the more he demanded and the less he thought of her. This is what she had seen of marriages she witnessed, and she had resolved to never sink to this level. But here she was. She sat up until midnight, changing channels looking for something to distract her, and eventually fell asleep on the couch.

The following day, she could not get running water in the taps and she was told by the gatekeeper that a water pipe had burst somewhere outside the estate. She was going to wait for Sean to come and help her find a solution but for now, she would drive to the gym and shower there. She hanged out at the gym for an hour then returned home. She sent Sean a text to inform him about the water problem and he said he had a standby room reserved at the Mayfair hotel. Xandra was to drive there and they would meet at the reception. When she arrived, he took her to the restaurant to eat and have tea before going to the apartment. At the apartment, she was impressed with the plan and décor and as she looked around, she took a peek at the fridge and the only thing in there was a tub of yogurt, open with a spoon in it. At close examination, she saw the rim covered in lipstick. It felt as if a knife went through her heart. She wasn't hit with jealousy but pain. She called Sean and showed it to him. "Who was your guest?" "No guest. That could be my ex-wife trying to scare women away." "Ahh! How does she know where you would go?" Xandra asked not wanting to make him uncomfortable but intent on getting to the bottom of the matter. "She doesn't wear lipstick but is capable of something like that. Yesterday, she shouted at me when I went there, and I left angrily and came here. I always came here when I left the house, and she brings the children to see me when they miss me." Xandra did not believe this. She knew it was a fabricated lie and she needed to run! *But where shall I go now that I am seven months pregnant, and my contract expired? My child will never grow up with her dad."* Her heart sank as she remembered a confidant telling her "He will trap you with a child!". Xandra had not believed it possible but here she was. She took a shower and got into the bed determined to survive this as she figures out what to do. He made passionate love to her and she consoled herself that he loved her after all. He brought her to his secret retreat cave. *I shall make sure I have another child close after this one so they can be of the same father and can grow up together. Then if we part ways I won't have to have children from different men.* Decided Xandra. A new agenda came into play.

17

"Accountability breeds response-ability." —Stephen Covey

A beautiful baby girl was born on 1 August. Sean fussed over Xandra so much that she felt she was his world again. He seemed to know everything about babies and was advising her how to handle and hold and breastfeed. All the friends and relatives that came to the hospital were impressed by the doting father and glowing mother. The baby girl, Zoe, resembled her mom. Xandra believed this marriage had added a major stone to the foundation.

Months later, as Xandra struggled with weight loss and getting into shape, she was not allowed to run on the road or to join the gym because men would see her and get indecent thoughts. Sean came home one evening with a bag of clothes which were very beautiful but because of the weight gain, they hiked to slightly one centimeter above the knew and he protested that she was naked. "You must not wear clothes that stop at the knee or hike above. Xandra was not amused but kept silent. Next, he came home with an affidavit that Xandra was his customary wife. He assigned to her his surname! Xandra was flattered but because she knew it was not legitimate, she felt shame at the same time. She did not protest and let it pass.

Sometimes Sean would be gone for days and did not offer excuses or explanations. Xandra would worry about it but make excuses for this behavior. When family members were visiting this situation would prove very embarrassing because they would want to know where Sean was and where he lived. Many times, when he didn't answer her calls she would press him for a reason. "Why do you think of the worst? Should you give me the benefit of the doubt in case I was in trouble someplace?" Xandra believed that to be true and resolved to give him the benefit of the doubt. She also realized that the late-night meetings would be indefinite and a preferred lifestyle.

Sean started arriving at unexpected times at home, luckily, he had brought a professional chef so meals and his shoes were no longer an issue. On arrival, Xandra would pick up baby Zoe and run to the door to meet him. He would arrive with an air of cheer but haughty. One day he asked "why do you always shove the baby in my face at the door when you should meet me and settle me first? Don't you know that is how our culture is? I need to send you to my mother for some lessons. When the child is grown and leaves home who will be left? What will you become of our relationship which you must nurture now?" Xandra was crushed. In her opinion, the three of them were a complete gift. Then Sean started accusing her of paying more attention to baby Zoe than to him! This time she called to confide in her mother. "That is how men are, my girl! They compete with children, and you must give him attention first and enjoy your children after. A man's needs come first." Said her mother with a light laugh of amusement. "That makes me so inadequate mom! I shall try." Xandra determined to work harder. Sadly, the friendship between her and Sean seemed to have thawed. He felt like the "boss" who had to be served. This was not her initial vision. She hoped they would remain friends. She wanted a friend, a lover, a business partner, a leader, and a protector in her husband. It dawned on Xandra that caregiving had become something she had to do more out of pressure orf obligation than of love.

18

"A friend loveth at all times, and a brother is born for adversity." – Proverbs 17:17 NIV

The call came very early the morning just as Xandra was getting down to pray. "Hey, Xandra. Have you heard from mom yet? Dad is very ill; he has kidney failure. He is very upset because the doctor told him he cannot have a kidney transplant at his age and is going to die," said Shafiq her big brother. Shocking and sad as the news was, the two siblings chuckled at the thought of that last statement and imagination of their father's reaction. "Send him to me. The medical systems here are so much more efficient and we can decide what to do." "But the medical costs will be huge," retorted Shafiq. "I know! We shall do the best we can and you all must chip in. Anyway, let me ask Sean for advice and call you back." Sean wasn't home. Xandra did not hesitate to call him. All consideration and fear aside, she dialed the number he had given her. "Hello, darling. You are up early. Is everything alright?" asked a sleepy Sean. Xandra was relieved he could pick up and talk freely. "Sean, my dad is very ill, kidney failure and high blood pressure; and they cannot treat him in Mbabane. I have suggested they send him to me because he trusts me and the medical services here. And sweetie, be strong. Dad is a strong man. He is going to be alright." "Oh, shame! Please tell them to organize and send him to Johannesburg. Let me call my friend Dr. Sussman, a nephrologist, to alert him. Can they send to us a medical report that the surgeon can work with?". "Sean, you are a blessing. I shall get that and ask them to get him ready to come."

Xandra drove to the airport alone and waited 3 hours before she saw her parents arrive. Her dad was in a wheelchair, looking pale but stoic. His wife walked next to him, cheerful as usual. A flight attendant was pushing the wheelchair while Mica pushed the luggage trolley. Xandra felt relief that Mica was with them because he always made her laugh. The two of them were forever friends and playmates. She would have help with driving and nursing. "I hear Sean is in Mauritius. I would have loved to find him here." Said Mr. Shafiq after salutations. He was so cheerful, it was comforting.

After her parents had settled in, Xandra poured a whiskey for Mica and a wine for herself and her mom and they sat by the fireplace discussing medical plans and family matters. "Zoe is exceptionally beautiful. I was hoping you would bring her home sooner so we can baptize her." Said her mother. "We are working on that mom Soon Sean will get his divorce and then we shall have holy matrimony." Xandra responded. "My child, it pains me and your father that you are living in sin. When will you and Sean get married?" asked her mother. "Tell her mom!" shouted Mica amused and trying to lighten the mood. Xandra knew this subject would arise at some point, but she wasn't ready for that now since she had not dared to push the matter with Sean. With all that was expected of her from Sean, she didn't want to fight over this issue. Therefore, she didn't have an answer for her parents. This made her very angry and she agitatedly replied "it is complicated right now ma. We shall talk more about it tomorrow." "Don't leave it too long my child. And don't give your brother any more drink or he will sing through the night and disturb his father. I will see you at the diner." She said as she got up to leave.

The truth of the matter is that in her struggle to align Sean's expectations to her dream, their relationship had become a sort of routine uncomfortably. She was neither fulfilled nor excited anymore. She was expectant though. She believed Sean was a man of noble character and would fulfill his promise to traditionally ask her parents for her hand in marriage and have a church wedding as expected.

Holy matrimony for Sean and Xandra had taken into the shadows because the romance was wearing off. The grim realities of life had come to roost. Sean's wife had fled to the USA, abandoning the children to him and they needed him with them. His business was not doing so well, his debtors had taken him to court and several of his fancy vehicles had been repossessed. Xandra's dad needed to have dialysis twice a week and paid in cash because he did not have medical insurance. The house they rented was luxurious and cost a lot. There was a lot of stress and strain on the new relationship at a very early stage. Yet, Sean was attentive and went all out to spend on her father's treatment. Having to tackle these problems together sort of bound them together for a season of difficulty. There was a time when Sean was being sought by the police with an arrest warrant for not court orders. Xandra was instrumental in hiding him and this shared difficulty was another exciting ride because they had a cause to fight together. Xandra felt like a heroine with a shared identity with Sean.

"Now, Xandra, your mother and I have been confronted by the clan elders who want to know when you are going to make things right and have the sacrament of Holy Matrimony with Sean. I have taught you about your ancestry. You have been raised to fear God. It is a disgrace to take up residence with a man to whom you are not officially married. We love Sean very much. I have been told that I might not have long to live. Although I intend to shame the doctors and outlive them, I would like to leave with a clear conscience that my daughter has honored God and her family. When are you two getting married?" Xandra's father asked. Xandra adored her dad and was always very blunt with him. He was the stricter of the parents, yet she found him easier to talk to. He had a way of listening and pondering what he was told, then would revert with a wise response in the form of parable, proverb, or captivating story. "Dad, things are still complicated because Sean has not divorced yet. He says he will do it in time and must wait a three years separation period before he can file. It will take some time. I am sorry for the shame I am bringing on the family." "You must ensure proper marriage, my child. The courts will legalize your union but will safeguard it; while the church will always help you fight to honor the covenant you make before God. And you must baptize this child soonest." With that, her dad got up, laid his hand on Xandra's head, patting her, and walked to his bedroom.

That night, Xandra prayed a special kind of prayer. She was ashamed of her relationship status. She was afraid to lose her father. She was insecure because she was financially dependent on Sean. She did not pray by the book but from the heart. Her prayer was sincere. *"In the name of the Father, the Son, and the Holy Spirit, I pray. Please God, help me. I have messed up again. Please show me the way out of this mess. Help Sean to do the right thing. Help him with money to pay his debtors and for the hospital. I still need my father, LORD. Let me see all my children come and walk me down the aisle when I get married. I know I keep messing up, please forgive me. Help me, LORD. Glory be to the Father, the Son, and the Holy Spirit. As it was in the beginning, is now and ever shall be. Amen"* Her prayers were getting more to the point and earnest.

Like Xandra's dad always said "a friend who stands by you in adversity is the true friend. Anyone can come to the party." Sean's care and attention, financial help, and advice were greatly appreciated by the patient, family, and friends. He was praised and honored even at home. Mention of Sean warmed people's hearts and aroused feelings of gratitude for apparently "saving" the life of a much loved and revered patriarch.

19

"Oh, what a tangled web we weave, when first we practice to deceive!" -Sir Walter Scott

"Hurry Sean, dad is dying. We are losing the battle." cried Xandra on phone. Hang on darling I am on my way. It had been a year since Xandra's dad had come to Johannesburg and was stabilized and sent home on peritoneal dialysis. He was able to walk and go to church and clan meetings with the bag. He had not only contracted peritonitis but was found with advanced cholangiocarcinoma. The doctors had predicted eight weeks and it was accurate. Xandra was distressed because she wanted to get to him and see him alive. "Be strong darling, I shall get you and Zoe tickets to travel tonight, and I shall follow. I shall call you back with a confirmation." Sean stepped in as the knight in shining armor again.

A week later, Sean had not been able to come, and Mr. Rafiq was laid to rest. As Sean was esteemed and thanked for his care, he was awaited. It caused Xandra so much grief to explain why Sean could not come to the funeral the shame exceeded her grief. She knew he was struggling financially and to save his ego she could not tell anyone. He wasn't admitting to this fact either but eventually sent a last-minute eulogy to be read at the funeral. Xandra trusted Sean so much that she did not check the message before it was passed on to someone read. The message made her feel even more ashamed because it only highlighted and repeated how much his love of the barbequed meat would be missed." This message was obviously not written by Sean and even those who had met him knew him to be smarter than that. Xandra's sense of loss was heightened. She felt alone because she could not share her multifaceted shame. She was living a lie.

A person who refuses to acknowledge a lie that they perceive is just as bad as the liar. Such a person cannot consider themselves a victim but an accomplice. They can neither blame nor resent another for the deception. Right after the funeral, Xandra decided to leave and return to Johannesburg to seek consolation and deal with her grief and shame. Sean sent a driver to pick her up and was not available to come and see her, the whole week. She was devastated. Zoe was very ill, and the cook was in a drunken stupor. That frightened her.

Unfortunately, the difficulty of nursing her father and several other obstacles that kept Sean and Xandra was vanquished, and the thrill of the relationship dissipated. Xandra was now burdened with much hospital debt from her dad's treatment and pediatric care; and she needed to find a job despite Sean's protests. She felt a sense of emptiness as she realized that she had to take a stand to find normal. She was no longer besotted with him and would have runway if she had gotten an international posting to a family duty station. For now, she would focus on paying the hospital debts and get another child. She had taken to checking every three weeks and was disappointed for a while, but not too long.

Her pregnancy came at a time when she was struggling financially and very lonely, and still grieving the loss of her father. She needed her dad for times like this. She had stopped going to church over a year ago. Before that, she only went to church as an obligation to take her father who would never miss a Sunday service. She was woken up with "dad is waiting for you to take him to church." She would protest "he was in dialysis for hours yesterday, isn't he tired?" They would always get to church an hour early so he could go for confession. *"I wonder what these sins he confesses to every week are. He never goes anywhere or does anything to require confession."* She wondered.

Xandra got a job at last. It didn't pay as much as what she earned before but it was an administrative job that would help her pay hospital debts and some of her personal needs. This job was an open door to the familiar of social environment and purpose beyond homemaking. Sean grew more absent, and she grew lonelier but remained hopeful. She resolved not to nag or sound needy. He also became stricter with her dress code – no pants, no hugging clothes, and no shorts and jeans. She did not agree but obeyed because she didn't want him to repeat "you don't listen." She had heard the "you don't listen to me," tirade so much it felt like being pelted with stones each time. It was a put-down and false accusation, she knew well. It made her feel abased and inadequate.

Xandra found a book that her father had passed on to her two weeks before he left Johannesburg for the last time. It was titled "Brokenness". When he gave it to her, she was offended because she believed he was telling her she needed to be broken and she defied that. When she picked up, she scanned through a few pages and was captivated. She put the book down occasionally because the grief of what she had discovered, coupled with intense long-time stress and the shame, the fear, the disillusionment, and remorse overwhelmed her and came pouring out in tears. She cried for hours and days following that.

Ten months after her dad passed away, Xandra had a baby boy. She called him Mark after her favorite character in the Bible. Mark was delightful and a big consolation. She felt recompensed at the loss of her dad. For some odd reason, Xandra became very sentimental and was often beset by feelings of self-pity. She cried over anything and everything, pleasant or unpleasant. Mark was a very quiet baby. By now she was used to living alone with her babies and had a stream of nannies and a few relatives stopping by to stay.

The concept of 'brokenness' not only intrigued but haunted her. She felt broken because of her many trials. She needed someone she could be vulnerable with and that couldn't be a relative or colleague. She read the book over again and had a chat with a colleague who was a pastor as well. Pastor Isaac referred her to another colleague, Joy, who was married to a pastor of a Baptist Church. Joy invited Xandra to church on Sunday. She agreed to not only meet her need for church but not to disappoint Joy.

The church was only a 10 minutes' drive from her house, and she didn't know what to expect. She thought that she would be invisible as is often the case at a new church, but she was mistaken. She was welcomed warmly, and Lorena was whisked away by a friendly usher to Sunday school. The worship session was so beautiful and something about it made her cry. She wept through it. She was warmly welcomed along with the new attendees. When the sermon started, she worried "here comes nap time. It is going to be embarrassing to fall asleep and drool, and even fart in public." Xandra had never listened to an entire sermon even if it was half an hour long. Pastor Elijah was so captivating and humorous that he brought the scriptures alive, relating them to daily life and public incidents. The congregation laughed and responded to every point with enthusiasm and soon enough the service ended with an altar call. Xandra took the Altar call again for the umpteenth time. *"I can hardly wait for next Sunday"*, she thought.

Before leaving church on the first visit, Xandra signed up for their weekly Bible study session. Now she could read the Bible again.

Even after the altar call, Xandra was feeling broken. Worse still, she harbored a secret. She kept a façade of a happily married woman, but the man was not living with her full time but came left as he pleased. The neighbors and regular visitors asked and wondered why he was never home. Xandra made excuses for him, "The man is a hard worker. He has to do follow up work on the farm and his internet services company in other countries. His work is his joy. He is so good at it that it combines as a livelihood and a hobby." She was in a bind, it hurt and she wouldn't admit to what the implied, that this much absence from home was abnormal. The secret was a burden, and she felt as if the whole world knew it. She needed to find a way not to make it right for that was beyond her control, she thought, but to cover it up well.

20

Train up a child in the way he go,
And when he is old they will not depart from it.

~Proverbs 22:6 NKJV

The faith of our ancestors is strong and enduring. When a child is raised in a particular culture, faith and tradition, it does not matter how rebellious he or she gets, they will have a twig to hold onto when the river sweeps over them; a hiding place when the lighting strikes; a shelter from the storm; a voice to cry out to an ever-present listener and a way out of entrapment. Xandra prayed at waking and sleeping, when in distress and when lonely, when confused and when ashamed. Every time she woke up with anxiety and fear in the middle of the night she prayed. When she couldn't articulate her words, she cried "God, help me."

"LORD, right now I believe that I sold my soul to the devil. I am suffocating here. I see myself in a box and don't know how to get out. I feel so alone. I am far away from my family and have no one to show me how to be a homemaker. These criteria of a virtuous woman are impossible. I haven't been able to get income out of my investments. I handle a lot of money but it gets finished so quickly, I cannot save. I am not allowed to join Curves, a women-only gym because Sean does not trust me. That hurts so bad because I want him to see me for who I am – loyal and faithful. He doubts my love when I live for him. He has made another friend, Zandile, and they exclude me in their rendezvous. He tells me that she is jealous of me and a bad person when he should be protecting and defending me. He hangs out with a woman friend he calls a sister even though they are not even remotely related, but I cannot have friends. I can't even allow new friends close because my family situation is so tense, I don't want anyone to see my struggles." Xandra confided prayer while window shopping at the Mall of Africa.

Sean was now spending a lot of time and traveling with Zandile. She was beautiful and caring. She was well connected and smart so he said she was introducing him to potential investors. He started leaving home early and return late. One day, Xandra little Mark tried to take pictures with Sean's phone and brought it to mom. When Xandra scanned through the photos, he found some intimate one between Sean and Zandile. There were photos of fun times hanging out in Zandile's garden drinking wine, wine tasting in Cape Town vineyards, pausing together at office parties, and a party within Johannesburg to whom Xandra was neither invited nor told about. She was heartbroken. After all, she had been through, she still believed Sean had the decency not to be unfaithful to her with a mutual friend. She made an attempt to confront him and he insisted it was business and all else was imagined. Xandra asked "what happened to our friendship? You don't talk about business and politics with me anymore." He didn't hesitate to boldly retort "you have nothing relevant to say." Despite years of emotional battering, Xandra still knew she was smart and had a lot to offer. This level of cruelty was not acceptable and she resolved the friendship was over. She would never engage him in conversation like they used to have. She would not expect it anymore. *"From this moment I will not miss the friendship, and we shall talk family business on a needs basis. I shall do my own thing, pursue my very talented and God-loving friends I have found. I will no longer entertain Zandile nor acknowledge her anymore."* A special bond was broken. Xandra did not care for how long she would endure or what her next move was. She had children to raise and career to revive. But first, she would apply to pursue higher education because she has been out of the workplace for seven years and had no confidence to seek employment. Besides, qualifications lose relevance, she had been told by a human resources officer in her previous workplace. While raising her children she would self-improve and make the best of the situation after all Sean was always gone.

Sean was a gardening expert. He was knowledgeable about a lot of things including cooking. He always trained and taught but his way of correcting was with mockery and criticism and abusive language. He had no qualms swearing in front of the children. Xandra was not argumentative but didn't hesitate to defend herself when attacked. He hated it when she explained or gave a reason for his criticism of comments. She grew increasingly defensive and it didn't help much.

Years of hanging out with children had moved Xandra to resort to television. She loved the movies but found herself nearly addicted to sitting long hours in front of the tv, changing channels frequently. She always said, *"the television sees me and speaks to me!"* When Sean was home, she spent every hour of the day serving him – ensuring his laundry was taken care of, shoes polished, sandals in place, towel changed, travel bags cleaned, meals done to his preference and no one made noise, every item was in its place. A day of its kind ended when Sean got into bed and then she took an hour or two to unwind in front of the tv or to read a book in the lounge. Often she had feet in a warm tub of water. This infuriated Sean. He despised her love for movies and reading. He called her a textbook mother and wife. *"I don't want a textbook wife and mother he said."* Many times when he wanted to make an impact he chose words that cut below the belt. She had cried at *"beautiful women are not to be married. You are not fit to be a mother. You are not fit to be a wife, and more."* Xandra knew better than to argue with him. She wouldn't bear it if she was to be beaten up for something she said. She resolved to never be respectful to him and to cover up so the children do not lose respect for their father and could grow in a seemingly happy home.

She had two new prayers *"LORD, please keep Sean away longer. If he has to come please let him come in peace because his children need him."* The other prayer was when Sean had been home about a week and started acting up and stressing her and the children. It went like this: *"LORD, in the name of Jesus, it is time for Sean to leave. Please find him work to do or give him a reason to leave soonest."*

It turned out that the days that Sean came home became stressful because of his demands. She felt she could barely exhale. Even the housekeeper and gardeners felt the tension because he would criticize and mock and belittle them. He ensured everybody felt his superiority. The day when he left home to go to work and travel abroad, was the best. Every time he drove out, Xandra would either go window shopping and treat herself at a café or make popcorn and sit for hours in front of the television just relishing the freedom. It was like the relief one gets emptying the bladder after holding it for a strenuous long time. The moment to exhale.

21

"Come, let Us go down and confuse their language so they will not understand each other. So the Lord scattered them from there over all the earth, and they stopped building the city. That is why it was called Babel—because there the Lord confused the language of the whole world. From there the Lord scattered them over the face of the whole earth."

— Genesis 11:7-9 NIV

We may be tempted to think that when we succeed in doing things, God has sanctioned it and so we are sufficient in ourselves, our learning, technology, skill, intellect sophistication, networks, and social standing, hence no longer need to ask, trust or commit our plans to God and obey Him. As with the Tower of Babel self-sufficiency is a delusion. People with utopian ambitions have fallen into the trap of arrogance and self-sufficiency. Many lives have ended up in ruin; the children suffering for the sins of the parents.

A time came when Sean told off Xandra for waking up to pray at night and for reading the Bible in the morning. He told her, "I resented Camilla for watching Christian tv networks and playing Christian radio in the home. Every time we quarreled, she ran to the kitchen and switched-on gospel music loudly. Even the children were upset because she spent too much time on it. What happened to you? When I met you, you did not pray as much or read the Bible? Now all you talk about is God!" Well, when you know what happened to your predecessor, you don't get overwhelmed when it happens to you. *"I shall have to be tactful about my prayer and Bible study times. I shall do more of it when he is out or sleeping."* And so, she did. However, Lorena and Mark so desired to stay up longer and they begged Xandra to let them read the Bible with them. They started listening to a children's audio Bible in a year program while reading along in their Bibles. They had nearly completed the entire Bible when Sean found out one evening. He was furious. "I can't stand you and your God! Now you are making my children read the Bible too!" Xandra was too shocked to respond. He didn't even allow her to respond but stormed out of the house. *Who on earth did I marry? I thought he believed in and feared God.!"* She wondered, sadly. *Could two people be more unequally yoked?*

When Sean returned that night, he reeked of alcohol and had a lot to say. She had nothing to say. At an opportune time, she jumped out of bed and went to the dressing room, locked the door behind her, got on her knees, and cried to the LORD. She didn't know what to ask of God but pleaded "help me, LORD. I have been foolish, disobedient, and offended you greatly. Do not let me be put to shame. And please God, give me an extra dose of love, mine is depleted. Help me so I may not disgrace you." There was an attempt to open the door and when he found it closed, Sean called out "darling are you praying?" "Hold on, I am coming." When she opened the door, he was grinning cheekily. "I know when you lock the door these days you must be praying. Come to bed darling." There were no apologies. She meekly followed him to bed and attended to his knees even as her heart ached. When he had had his satisfaction, she turned around and curled up, and wept quietly. She could hear him breathing heavily as he fell asleep, oblivious of her pain. She tried in vain to sleep and after a while, a song she didn't know that she knew rose in her spirit *"the glory and lifter of my head, the glory, and lifter of my head. O thou O LORD are a shield for me, the glory and lifter of my head."* That chorus kept running in her head and she remembered hearing it on the radio. She got curious enough to get up and check if these were from the Bible. She knew that God was speaking to her. She was consoled, and went back to bed, letting her spirit sing the chorus until she slept.

Sean had defined himself as a man who professed to know God but did not fear or love Him. Xandra's commitment to having a closer relationship with God grew. She realized that she prayed most when trouble arose. Then it occurred to her that if she remained connected to God, she would not be shaken when trouble arose. It was better to stay connected than to run to God every time an emergency arose. And she did. She studied the scriptures more, prayed more, joined a church cell group, and even committed to the church membership at Fourways Christian church. It was at this time that she got baptized by immersion.

The worst situation is when you know what the problem is but do not dare to take a stand against it. When you have handed your reigns over to another human being, you feel incompetent to do a lot of things and that includes making the right judgment and decisions. *"Life isn't worth living like this. I don't want to face the day anymore." Observed Xandra. "Maybe I should just starve myself to death in that way I will be able to take care of the children until the end. Starting today, I won't eat and even now I shall go to bed until it is time to go pick the children from school." She thought.* Sean had left that morning and now she wasn't obliged to fuss over homemaking. She walked into the bedroom at 09:00 am and drew the curtains then changed into a robe and jumped into bed. She was feeling tired but could not fall asleep. A thought came to her *"you used to fast for 40 days while working. Why don't you do that instead of starving to death?"* Her heart quickened with the memory, a new solution. She made up her mind to start with immediate effect. With that, Xandra got out of bed and went to cook, to prepare for the children. That was a lifesaving revelation.

In her gratitude journal that night, Xandra had a lot to be grateful for. She had kept a gratitude journal for the last 12 years. She resolved to put her writings in the form of gratitude very night and prayer rather than complaints. It is hard to feel grateful when our hearts are broken, and our dreams are dashed. There is always something to be thankful for. Once when undergoing a lot of stress and profound loss, she forced a litany of thanks and made as many as fifty because she felt that is the only way to mourn and find cheer. Thanksgiving for Xandra always followed naked, complete bitter surrender to sorry and pain, tears, and pleas. She did believe God loved her. She had a track record of miraculous answers to prayer and was certain she would be rescued from this pit she was in. On some days she could only write just five. Every time she was greeted and responded, "I am fine", she meant it because she was grateful.

Alas! The two builders have different needs, different motivations, spoke a different language, believed different things, and were no longer facing the same direction together. Sean's control over Xandra was complete with a subjugated wife who no longer served him out of love but fear. She stopped protesting loudly and wrote letters appealing for justice, seeking to understand. The letter helped her vent but did not make an impact.

22

*And let us consider how we may spur one another on toward love and good deeds, **25** not giving up meeting together, as some are in the habit of doing, but encouraging one another—and all the more as you see the Day approaching.*

– Hebrews 10:24-25 NIV

An African proverb says, "he who chases you, shows you the way." When Sean had shown he would never be appreciative of who Xandra was or what she did and how she related to God, it left one choice and that is what she took. She chose to honor God in everything she did. "I shall serve as unto the LORD. I shall perform for an audience of one, Jesus Christ. As long as I have not done anything to offend and disobey God, I will do what I deem right for me.

Xandra was invited to a baby shower by her relatives and the venue was of another relative whom she had not connected with because she kept her walls of privacy and self-protection up. This was the first event she attended in three years and whilst there, she met some really fun people. During the same week, she was invited to attend a Bible study focusing on "The Virtuous Mother, Wife, Homemaker." This was a passageway to spiritual growth, social exposure, and much support. She remained private but now had more invitations to other invitations – baby showers, spring celebrations, birthdays, and motivational talks. Xandra was also requested to participate in serving, cooking, and giving talks, leading prayers and dedications. She felt accepted, included, and found purpose outside her family setting. God of grace had not forsaken her.

This was not without resistance. At first, Sean wanted to meet all her friends. On her forty-first birthday, her friends threw a party at her house, and Sean arrived that day with lots of wine and chocolates and was overly impressed by the the setup her friends had made. He excitedly opened various wines and champagne and poured for the ladies. When the party was over and the visitors had left, Sean noticed with shock that none of the glasses had been touched. "These ladies don't drink? They even left before midnight!" Xandra responded with pride "Not all of them. They don't make alcohol the center of the fun. They all don't stay out late because they are married." Both Sean and Xandra had never known a party where alcohol was not consumed and in large quantities. Xandra was being deliberately celebrated and she felt loved and honored. Somehow, Sean was at ease because as much as he dreaded new friends for her, he felt different about this lot. They were a different kind of woman, and he sounded like he could entrust his wife around them.

Xandra's church cell group was composed of ladies older than her and very mature spiritually. It is with them that she realized that it was a gift from God, for all, to speak in tongues. Connie and Jules prayed fervently for her to receive the gift of the Holy Spirit motivated her. On the first occasion, she was overcome with a feeling of intense love and so much laughter. This was the first time she heard of the spirit of joy. How amazing that Holy Spirit would touch her like that and make her laugh uncontrollably with tears streaming down her face. She didn't think she was deserving! Xandra wanted more.

23

"The purpose of life is not to be happy. It is to be useful, to be honorable, to be compassionate, to have it make some difference that you have lived and lived well." Ralph Waldo Emerson

"How could you start looking for a job without telling me? Don't you know that I do not agree and that alone is why you won't be employed by anyone? You won't even make money from your real estate because I, your husband, have not allowed it." Sean gloated. "Let's just have another baby since you have time on your hands." Xandra protested "how can you think like that? The doctors say it is dangerous to get pregnant at my age. Besides we have many children already. You and I don't even go out together; you don't do fun stuff with me or take me traveling as you promised. I need to pick up and rebuild my career." Sean was in a more amicable mood and did not get angry but instead tried a businessman angle "I have been invited to my business acquaintance's fiftieth birthday party in Maputo. We can go together. Then you can have that baby." "Sean, darling, do you mean that? I shall be grounded raising another baby. Anyway, Lorena and Mark are too busy for me but have been asking for a child -Mark wants a baby brother while Lorena wants a sister."

Feeling purpose and most of all flattered that Sean still desired to be with her in a family way, Xandra set to dreaming about the baby. *"I know this is his way of keeping me trapped and busy. But I do want a baby. I wanted four to six children and had given up. It doesn't what the doctor says because in my family we don't have complications and abnormalities. Women deliver healthy babies into the early fifties like my eldest sister Gonza."*

It was a lonely pregnancy. Xandra signed up with a gynecologist who was very kind and seemingly Christian. However, she discovered that Dr. Mugo would always forget her name, and a few times instead of checking the baby on the obstetrics scan, she would bring her equipment set to have a pap smear test. Xandra decided to get another doctor. She was only allowed female gynecologists, so she got one, Dr. Young, who seemed pessimistic and kept giving her bad reports about the baby. She even predicted that the pregnancy would not end well. Xandra wrote her off as a non-Christian and from the looks of her style of dress, she was probably in the dark arts. She surmised. Nevertheless, she retained and prayed even more. Every time she got a bad report from Dr. Young, she would not tell anyone for fear of repeating the negative and bringing it to pass. She would instead pray about it and then a week go to Dr. Jones expecting good news, and that is what she got. Xandra enjoyed being pregnant because it made her sleepy and lazy but this one found her very alert and creative. She signed up for a second degree.

"I didn't permit you to study. You have to give all your attention to the family," said Sean when he found out. "It is a distance learning study with the University of South Africa and won't take my time from family care. If it is about money, it did not cost a lot." Sean was visibly angry. "If you continue to study, I am going to take my children away." He threatened. Xandra got furious but chose not to display it. *"This time he has gone too far. I will not put up with this cruelty."* Instead, with calm resolve, she told him "I know you love them as much as I do. You can take them." That was the bravest she had ever been with Sean. Xandra remembered a saying that she grew up hearing, that *"If you compromise with a witch, he will eat your children."*

Baby Zoe was born on 9 September, healthy, 3100 grams. Sean had been away and arrived an hour after the delivery. Xandra had gone to the hospital and bought herself flowers for her room, set up her speakers for music, and unpacked her bags. She didn't ask her friends to come and be with her because she was embarrassed to admit Sean wouldn't be there. She no longer felt needy and had accepted, albeit with much sadness that her needs were not Sean's priority. She was happy when he arrived because someone had to do the school runs and ensure Lorena and Mark would be brought to see their sibling.

24

"Fool me once, shame on you; *fool me twice,* shame on me." – Stephen King

No one will ever know why he did it, but while on a trip abroad, Sean called Xandra and told her that he wanted to now marry her officially. "I want us to have that church wedding you have always wanted, after all the traditional ceremonies to honor your family." The month leading to this pledge had been tense, and Sean was distant and aloof. "Sean? How did you come up with that at this time?" "I have been thinking of you since I left home and want to put things right, my darling." She pressed to confirm tactfully, "Shall I tell my friends and family?" "Yes! By all means. We need to get someone to book the venues in Mbabane. Don't worry, I have a friend working there, I shall ask him to book and send us the quotations. I am coming home in three days, and we can plan some more." With that, Xandra knew that if he was playing with her, he would not let her tell people because it would disgrace him not to honor his word.

Xandra announced to her mother and called up all her siblings and friends. Her friends were her prayer team. The latter did not know that she wasn't legally married to Sean yet. They were all very excited because amongst them were professional bakers and event organizers. The children were most excited and started planning with her too. Xandra was apprehensive though. Sean had let her down in many other things and she was cautious not to be jubilant about it. He could easily say let us wait for an opportune date and not do it. When asked to go check out dresses, she refused, saying they must wait until she had gotten into shape. When Xandra announced Sean's plans for holy matrimony, her mother asked her, has he been formally divorced. When he writes asking for a date to visit the family for the traditional ceremony, he should attach it. Xandra's heart sank. She knew her mother was right but how was she going to tell that to Sean without upsetting the cart?

When Sean arrived, he was in a happy mood. He knew how to sweep Xandra off her feet because every time he was in good temperament, she forgot all the pain and enjoyed herself. Later, after diner, as they chatted and started to plan, Sean wanted to know whom she had told and how they reacted. Xandra told him, "You need to ask your father to write to my family asking for a date to come and ask for my hand officially. Mom says you should attach a copy of your divorce certificate." "Of course, I shall ask my lawyer to get that for us. You know Camilla is in Zambia and we don't know her address so the summons was sent there…" Xandra lost interest in hearing anymore because she knew this was it. They would wait forever to have that promised wedding. For several months to come, emails from hotels and caterers sending quotes and following up came to her mailbox. A sad reminder of another broken promise. Her prayer partners asked over the years "what happened to that planned wedding?" She did not make excuses or lie this time but told them "Waiting for Sean to sort himself. He doesn't talk about it anymore."

"When will I ever learn?" cried Xandra. She had read a saying by Pierce Brown, that "Liars make the best *promises.* "I wonder what they would say of those who fall for those lies every time." All that Xandra cared about was to have peace and survive the emotional abuse until a time when she would find a way out. She was not in a hurry. The children were young and needed a father, even if he did not know how to play and engage them. He spoilt them with expensive gifts and everything they wanted. He gave to them generously even if he had nothing left with him. That was a very endearing trait of his. Xandra had ways of fighting pain by turning the blame on herself. *"It isn't his fault we are in this situation. I allowed myself to dream and believe him. My desires got me into this sticky mess. I forgive him. Here we are in this beautiful home that we have designed, built, and furnished ostensibly. One day, God will put things right. I pray about it. God is faithful to deliver us."*

25

They claim to know God, but by their actions they deny him. They are detestable, disobedient and unfit for doing anything good." - Titus 1:16 NIV

When Zoe was about 3 years old, Xandra had a lot of praying friends, then decided to invite some, with young children, to form a praying mothers' group. This group started meeting in her home once a month, for two hours every evening. If it so happened that Sean was at home, he fussed and complained and demanded her attention. She persisted with the prayer meetings for about two years. He despised this meeting and complained that she prioritized her friends over her family; she was making the family uncomfortable with praying in the house. Xandra knew she would never hear the end of it but was not about to disband the praying mothers' group. She needed this prayer meeting in her house because she felt it reinforced a holy altar and would bless her home. Sean had to get what he wanted, so he started leaving the house as the praying moms arrived and would return just before midnight. When she did not feel bad about it, he decided to accuse her of disrespect. Xandra could not understand how hosting a praying team at home once a month for two to three hours could be interpreted as such. She did not respond or react or make false apologies. Sean complained to the children and tried to enlist their support by telling them that these praying mothers were not family friends and they were invading family space. "They are confining us to one wing of the house and imposing their prayers on us." He complained.

"Xandra, as your husband and head of the household I am telling you not to bring your prayer group home anymore. You can meet them elsewhere." She listened to his rambling and asked, "don't I have a right to invite my friends to this home?" "You can meet them elsewhere, in one of their homes, and not at ours." Xandra decided not to go against him. "He is fighting God, not I, and shall reap the consequences of kicking prayer out of our home." She was flabbergasted. *What is it about prayers and the Bible that makes this man uncomfortable? I kept secret the baptism of Lorena and Mark from him because he opposed it. And now he is not afraid to go against God?* Sean seemed to compete with God. The children wanted to know what Xandra would do; if she would resist or obey. "I will not disobey your dad. I shall hold the meeting elsewhere." The asked, "Is dad a Christian mommy?" She responded, "He just needs more of Jesus that is all." Every month on the same prayer day, the praying mothers found a cake shop with a private meeting room and continued to pray together.

Weeks later, Sean went on a rampage finding fault, criticizing, and constantly telling Xandra that she did not respect him. He seemed to be looking for every opportunity to draw her into a quarrel and she cautiously evaded him. At one of those times, as she changed Zoe into pajamas, Sean came up to them, leaned into her face, and announced, *"I hate you more and more."* These words hit her hard because even though she felt the absence of love, she did not know the intensity of his feelings. She remained expressionless and nodded her head in acknowledgment. "I see! Now I know how you hate me. It is well." With that she finished dressing up Zoe and gave Sean a wide berth as she left the bedroom, feeling shocked and sad. *How did we get this far? What did I do to this man to drive him to hatred?* She proceeded to serve diner. Zoe arrived first and refused to wash her hands. "Leave me alone mommy" she shouted. Xandra walked up to her, picked her up, and took her to the sink to wash. She started shouting in protest, as Sean was taking his seat. When she had finished washing her hands, Zoe ran to the table crying "mommy is mean to me!". As Xandra approached the table, a plate came flying at her and hit her in the sheen. She was shocked that Sean had don that to her. She got furious and knew she had to do or say something, at the same time was sure he would hit her if she shouted at him. Xandra continued to the table and picked up her plate with its food and threw it to the floor then looked brought her face to Sean and told him sternly, "this time you have gone too far. I shall report this abuse to the police." She walked away towards the bedrooms to figure out her next move. By the time she got to the bedroom, she knew she could not share a bed with someone who felt this way about her and was capable of violence. She decided to move all her belongings out of the room to a spare bedroom and set up there. She took a change of clothes, toiletries, and her Bible and journal out first. Before she could make her bed, grief overwhelmed her and Xandra allowed herself to cry. She wept until she heard footsteps, then pretended to be busy. When Lorena and Mark peeped at the door, she smiled at them, as their faces crumbled. They started to cry, and she joined in the party. "Why did dad behave like that mommy? It was Zoe's fault!" cried Lorena. "Is he a Christian mommy? I always wanted to be like dad but now I don't know" said Mark in a shaky voice. Xandra collected herself and did just what her mother would expect of her. "Children, this is between your dad and I. It is not Zoe's fault. What dad did was very wrong, but I forgive him." "But mom, you and dad have been unhappy for so long, why are you still together? You let him treat you with disrespect and get away with it each time." Lorena sounded disgusted and angry at her mother. "Children, your dad is a special person. He loves you very much. Even big people disagree and sometimes feel like they don't like each other. Then they reconcile." "Are you moving into this room mom?" "Yes! I shall move here until this matter is resolved. Both dad and I love you all very much. Let us pray for peace."

26

Three things you cannot recover in life: the word after it's said, the moment after it's missed, and the time after it's gone.

- Abdelnour, Ziad K

Towards midnight, Sean knocked on Xandra's door. She ignored it for half a minute and knew she had to deal with it. Sean was in pajamas. "Xandra, I am sorry. Please come to bed. We can talk about it there." She was expecting this and she nodded her head vigorously, deciding to lay out her case "first you announce how you hate me more and more. Then you hit me in the sheen with a plate and draw blood. Am I a sex object to you? I am not coming back to bed and in case you haven't noticed, I have taken off your ring." Sean moved forward into the room and she was forced to move. He moved and sat on her bed asking her to sit down so they can talk. Xandra sat down intending to state her stance. He listed all his grievances against her and insisted she had to go back to bed. "we shall make love and resolve this." This made her sadder. "Sean, I know that I cannot satisfy your demands ever. I never have and never will. Now that you hate me, there is nothing I will ever do that will satisfy you. I am done. I am not your sex object and because I am hurt, I cannot force myself to satisfy your needs. I won't do it. Now I have to sleep, please leave." "Alright, come and lie here next to me. Let me hold you awhile." Xandra felt angry and knew she couldn't get him out of the bedroom. She walked out, walked to the linen cupboard and took a spare blanket and went to the lounge, switched on the television, and sat until she heard Sean go to his room then quickly moved and locked her bedroom door. She did not sleep that night, feeling relieved that she had succeeded not to be forced to have sex against her will and that she had a chance to make changes to this relationship. Xandra had cried hard with every discovery of infidelity and those were many; and had resolved to let it go, acknowledge she was illegally in this relationship like all the other women. She had lost and would concentrate on what matters most – her children. Verbal, mental, and emotional abuse had hurt but she tolerated it. Physical abuse and the threat of it was the final stroke. She knew that once that started, if left to fester, it would get worse and as she told other women "once he threatens you, know that love is dead. When he hits you then he has abased you to a point where you are worth nothing to him."

She prayed through the Psalms and journaled until she couldn't keep her eyes open. The situation had gotten out of control. She sent Gonza, her big sister a text message relating her saga. She knew that if she told her mother she would be told to go to bed with her husband and work things out from there. There was something novel about being hit with a plate and she wanted to tell someone who would understand the implication of this. She sent messages to her closest friends Diana, Chipo, and Chrissie. It was not pity she was seeking but to deal with the reality that now she had officially completed the cycle of abuse.

The following morning, after taking the children to school, she went to church to talk to a counselor in the Hope Centre. She knew that Sean would be waiting for her to return so he can start convincing her all that happened was her fault. Not returning as expected would infuriate him and somehow it made her happy. The first stop was in the chapel where she journaled, prayed, and cried to the LORD for over two hours. She didn't have an appointment at the Hope Centre but Sue Wells, the Counsellor was gracious to listen to her for two hours. They prayed, and she concluded that even if she was living in a polygamous and adulterous relationship, he was not her husband. The scriptures indicated that when you slept with a man you became one. However, it was not the will of God to continue in adultery, she needed to deal with this matter first. Xandra returned home dissatisfied and not convinced she had a solution. She remembered the woman at the well to whom Jesus told "The fact is, you have had five husbands, and the man you now have is not your husband. What you have just said is quite true (John 4:18)." It is possible to live with a man as husband and wife and not belong to each other.

Xandra needed to triangulate her findings, so she remembered her friend Elizabeth who always told her the truth without fear. When she had recounted her woes to Elizabeth, she had told her "My sister in Christ, that man entered a covenant with another woman and broke it. God knows and recognizes the wife of his youth, and you are an intruder. She still spiritual authority over him. She has soul ties with him, and you will not be happy with him because he belongs to her. If you continue to pray for him to get saved, know that he will be required to return to the wife of his youth." "Oh Elizabeth, it is fifteen years and truly we haven't been happy. Everything he complained about his wife, I keep hearing said about me. My prayers have come back to me unanswered. God is not honoring this relationship. If only I could get a job to support myself and the children, I could get out of his life."

Sean left after three days to travel and insisted that when he gets home, he wanted his wife back in their bedroom. Sadly, he sounded entitled to sex with her whether she liked or not. Xandra started feeling bitterness, resentment, and regret. She started remembering every ugly word and deed she had suffered. By the fifth day, she realized that her joy was gone, and she couldn't conjure those feelings. She was alarmed to feel deep hatred rising. She did not want to ask God to give her an extra dose of love as she always did. She did not want to feel this way either. She had never in her life come to a point where all good had left her. It scared her. She called up Agape Healing and Deliverance Ministry that offers training and healing retreats. She was told that there was a healing retreat scheduled in three days. She signed up for it.

Sean arrived the night before the retreat. When he knocked on the bedroom door, she told him that she would tell him of her final decision after the retreat on Sunday. He flew into a fit "you don't need a shrink to tell you how to feel and what to do. We can sort this on our own. You cannot go that retreat because I haven't permitted you." "It doesn't change the fact that you hate me, and I don't feel any good at all. Goodnight Sean, you can take the children to school tomorrow, I shall take uber if you won't give me a lift there." "Xandra, I don't hate you. It just slipped out because frustrated with you." With that, he left her alone when he heard her resolve. "Whew! He did not stay pestering me to go sleep with him. My spiritual wellbeing is for me, and I don't need permission." She assured herself more to convince herself she was doing the right thing.

After the retreat, she felt better and was resolved to find a way out of the mess. Sean pestered her every night and one night walked into her room before she locked her door and pleaded until she gave in. She convinced herself that "he is providing of us therefore I have to give in to his demands until I can find the means to get out. He has my body and not my heart. God will understand that I don't have a choice, after all, I am not changing men but honoring this one as my husband." Even as she gave in, she knew that she would hate herself for that. She let him sleep in her new room that night and the following day, she felt like a martyr, moving back to their bedroom.

Xandra forgot to seek the LORD about her decision but took a convenient decision. She knew that all her problems arose from disobeying God and not considering God first in her decision. *"For the LORD gives wisdom; from his mouth come knowledge and understanding. He holds success in stores for the upright; he is a shield to those whose walk in blameless, for he guards the course of the just and protects the way of his faithful."* (Proverbs 2:6-8 NIV).

She knew that she was not being true to herself. But then, she had betrayed herself so many times over the years. She had false dignity, no self-esteem, and walked in fear of being exposed. Shakespeare wrote, "This above all: to thine own self be true, And it must follow, as the night the day, Thou canst not then be false to any man. Farewell, my blessing season this in thee!"

27

"But he must ask [for wisdom] in faith, without doubting [God's willingness to help], for the one who doubts is like a billowing surge of the sea that is blown about and tossed by the wind. For such a person ought not to think or expect that he will receive anything [at all] from the Lord, being a double-minded man, unstable and restless in all his ways [in everything he thinks, feels, or decides]. – James 1:6-9 AMP

Xandra has taken the popular decision to conveniently succumb to a relationship that she knew did not glorify God. She wasn't happy about it but it gave her relief from strife. She needed to hear a reprimand or encouragement when she called her Shafiq. "Sis, you know that it will get worse and not better. Did enquire of God first?" "No! but wouldn't God want for me to pursue peace?" she asked. "I honor the institute of marriage and it would make me happy if you and Sean could work things out. But you are going about this process the wrong way, with the wrong motivation. This is not the "straight and narrow'. Decisions made in fear do not spring from faith in God's ability to intervene. You are consulting me now because your conscience is accusing you. Beware, compromise is at the heart of disobedience and rebellion." Xandra hung her head in shame. She did not argue but listened intently. "So now you have gone and compromised for the sake of your peace and well-being of the children. I want you to get your Bible and let us read together Luke 9:24-26 and Matthew 10:37 and if you don't get your answer then I have nothing more to say." Beads of sweat broke out on Xandra's nose. She opened the Bible App on her phone and started to read aloud *"For whoever wishes to save his life [in this world] will [eventually] lose it [through death], but whoever loses his life [in this world] for My sake, he is the one who will save it [from the consequences of sin and separation from God]. For what does it profit a man if he gains the whole world [wealth, fame, success], and loses or forfeits himself? (Luke 9:24-26 AMP)."* Her she rubbed her nape as she paused to contemplate the clear truth she had read. *"why does Shafiq do this to me each time?"* she pondered. "Now read for us the next one but change the translation this time," he commanded. *"If you love your father or mother or even your sons and daughters more than me, you are not fit to be my disciples (Matthew 10:37 NLT)."* She knew the truth when she heard it. No truth hits home as hard as the Word of God.

Compromising her values and principles was not new and she knew it. For the entire six weeks that Sean was away, he called twice a day professing love and promising to make things right. Xandra was not sure if she still had hope in her or buying peace and time to raise the children because she no longer believed in Sean's promises. She knew that he did not love who she was but who he could make out of her. *"I deserve to be loved, protected, and accepted, yet I am lonely, unloved not knowing for how long this will go on,"* Xandra argued with herself. *"I need to find out what it is that is holding back my blessings. Either we are cursed, bewitched or God is angry at me. I am going to wage spiritual warfare with praying at every watch hour."* Xandra started on a journey of works, hoping to increase prayer power for results. She sought the LORD for what He could do and not for who He is. Embarking on a journey of intense fasting and prayer, making declarations, reciting prayer points every three hours of the day and night, Xandra got busy. Instead of finding peace and assurance, she got more desperate. Her focus was on her circumstances and not her walk. Just because she was faithful to her husband, loving to her children, prayerful, and engaging in the scriptures, she believed that she was in right standing with God.

Four years later, a frustrated and fatigued Xandra called on her friend, Pastor Kora to complain about how she had walked right, waged spiritual warfare unsuccessfully. "But why are you waging spiritual warfare in that way? Enough of that! Pray for blessings because Jesus redeemed you from the curse. You are busy praying what you do not have and complaining to God as if you do not believe that Jesus already obtained everything you ever need. Your prayer should acknowledge what you already have in Christ. When you focus your prayer on what you do not have, you pray a lie. You will not overcome a lie by embracing a lie but you overcome a lie by embracing the truth. That deception will keep you desperate and being rooted in a lie will drag on through your life. Embrace the truth that God already blessed you with every spiritual gift in the heavenly realm. Seek God and build a relationship with Him. Keep your eyes on Jesus, above the storms. You are sitting in heavenly places with Christ Jesus and the principalities and beneath you. You do not need to pray to open a portal so God can send your blessings to you on earth when you have dual citizenship. Bring what you have in the heavenly position to the earthly realm." Pastor Kora explained as Xandra's eyes widened with this revelation. "I had forgotten that I can pray for blessings. I used to believe I had the favor of God before I got born-again. Now when I should know better, I thought I had to do something to obtain the blessings! What a waste of time!"

28

"Keep on asking, and you will receive what you ask for. Keep on seeking, and you will find. Keep on knocking, and the door will be opened to you. – Matthew 7:7 NLT

During the Lenten fast, Xandra decided to fast for forty days to make more time with the LORD. This time she was not seeking intervention to solve her problems, but for intimacy with God. On the third morning of the fast day, after she had taken the children to school, she returned home and started her Bible study with worship. When she opened her Bible, it was to Galatians 5. Whereas in the past she skimmed over that chapter concentrating on the fruit of the spirit and nothing else. This time her scales fell off and the concepts of "freedom in Christ," the difference between walking in the flesh and the spirit became clear. As she read the list of the "acts of the flesh" she felt convicted and overwhelmed with intense sorrow. Holy Spirit's presence in that lounge was heavy as she fell to her knees remembering every sin that she had committed and forgotten, sins she had not recognized or intended, and sins of compromise. She realized that she had broken the ten commandments, the implication of which terrified and shamed her. Xandra started to weep, falling to her knees, she held her face in her hands as if someone was watching. As she recounted to her prayer group days later, "I was blind but now I see!" Xandra wept for a long time, pleading with God to forgive her in between sobs. She did not think that she deserved pardon and could not comprehend how God could bear to look at her. When she got off her knees, she turned to see herself in the mirror, still speaking to the LORD about her shame. The girl in the mirror looking at her was not the one she loved and admired. She saw in her eyes and mind the sins of the flesh, the disgraced, disgusting, filthy woman she believed she was. *"God, will you ever forgive me? she asked.* The response which she did not expect was quick "But that is why, I sent my son, Jesus, to die for you." *"I am unworthy"* she wept. *"I am a merciful God. Because you are undeserving, I extended grace to you."* The weeping increased as she fell to her knees in gratitude. "For the first time, I understand the sacrifice of Jesus for me. I now understand what Your grace means to me, LORD."

Xandra read Galatians chapter 5 again and again. She started confronting the obvious self-deception in her life. One such deception was her acceptance of the proposal for marriage while her husband was still married to his first wife. She took off the ring and put it away in disgust. *"What sort of woman knowingly accepts a marriage proposal from a married man and becomes a mistress?" She questioned her judgment.* She started journaling and did not stop until two hours later when it was time to go and pick up the children. She washed her puffy face and applied light makeup to disguise her misery. Then it occurred to her that she needed to start afresh and this included removing the hair implants and accepting herself the way God made her.

Confessing her sins to her children one was one of pulling the walls down to be authentic and seek accountability. By the time she was done recounting her issues, Mark was crying along with her. They each asked at different intervals "so mom you have been sinning against God all this time?" Lorena asked, "Did you have sex before marriage then?" "Yes, I sinned and now the LORD has made it clear to me, I confess those sins and repent." "Does dad know this?" inquired Mark. "Not yet. I shall let him know tonight. "I need to have a natural fresh start for renewal and would like to cut off my hair. Will you guys help me?" "O yes mom, I would love to cut your hair. But if I mess it up you will be laughed at!" Lorena announced enthusiastically. "That's alright. I can handle it."

That same evening, when the children had gone to sleep, Xandra called Sean. She was filled with much joy at finding out where she was at and deciding to walk right with God. "What does this imply darling? I hope you are not becoming fanatical about this Christian thing?" "No! Sean, God revealed to me how we have been walking in obedience. I am ashamed to finally face the truth that even though I tried to do things right, I had sinned greatly. To think that I broke all the ten commandments, and He still loves me. I am going to do right by God this time" Sean was quiet for a few seconds. "I think you should not do anything drastic until we talk this through. I have a series of meetings for the next three days. And darling, remember I do not agree with that fasting. We need to agree as a family." It was no use arguing with a man who thought he had to permit her to walk right before God and if and when she could fast. Xandra switched the microphone on and rested the phone on the armrest. She muted her phone and switched on the news. She knew very well that Sean's talking about his desires, his complaints, and his plans were just beginning. She did not have to hear it all over again. She turned to the faith channel to listen to worship. It was nine o'clock when the call began. She occasionally unmuted the phone just exclaim and give the "aha!" and "I get it" and "God, help us". This way Sean was satisfied that he had been heard. "Darling, I have an early meeting tomorrow. Take good care of our children. Good night." "Goodnight and God be with you" concluded Xandra.

"I know that I am to submit to my husband. He is not even my husband. I can disobey him if he wants to make me walk in sin. I have confessed and repented of my sins and will not grieve the Holy Spirit with compromise again. I have prayed through the home and shall get to the airport early to pray there too" resolved Xandra. She knew that what she dreaded the most will be the hardest to fight, and she would insist to share her bed. He felt and behaved entitled. She called Shafiq to air her views and seek his opinion.

"What you have decided is a good thing, Xandra. Have you asked God about this? I know He would not want you to make a prodigal of his child. "It is written that even if your husband does not believe or obey, he could be won over by the wife when they see your respectful and pure conduct" advised Shafiq. She knew Shafiq did not believe in the sustainability of her marriage anymore, but he intended to help her out in a godly way. "If you refuse him sex, which is his greatest need from you, you could be sending him out to sin by seeking it elsewhere." "Right, I hear you. I could not care less if he went to the street as long as he left me alone. I will only accede if forced." "God is waiting to hear from you, Xandra. Pray about it" Shafiq said. "I shall pray to God to hit him with impotence, so he does not defile me," Xandra said seriously. At this stage, the one thing that was keeping her in bondage and abuse was sex. Sean may have needed it, but he used it as a domination tool. *"There is something about sex that makes me feel used, weak, and brainless." Every time it incapacitates me and blinds me from the truth. It seems to enable fear and helplessness. It makes me feel like a subordinate and slave to his needs. One does not need to be in a physical chain to be in sexual bondage. But when did I, a child of God become a victim? Is it Sean's fault or my inability to resist?"*

29

"There are two sides to every issue: one side is right and the other is wrong, but the middle is always evil. The man who is wrong still retains some respect for truth, if only by accepting the responsibility of choice. But the man in the middle is the knave who blanks out the truth in order to pretend that no choice or values exist, who is willing to sit out the course of any battle, willing to cash in on the blood of the innocent or to crawl on his belly to the guilty, who dispenses justice by condemning both the robber and the robbed to jail, who solves conflicts by ordering the thinker and the fool to meet each other halfway. In any compromise between food and poison, it is only death that can win. In any compromise between good and evil, it is only evil that can profit. In that transfusion of blood which drains the good to feed the evil, the compromise is the transmitting rubber tube."— Ayn Rand,

The stage for compromise was set. Is there a godly way to compromise? Would she compromise by following 1 Peter 3:1 AMP *"In the same way, you wives, be submissive to your own husbands [subordinate, not as inferior, but out of respect for the responsibilities entrusted to husbands and their accountability to God, and so partnering with them] so that even if some do not obey the word [of God], they may be won over [to Christ] without discussion by the godly lives of their wives,?"* wondered Xandra.

Xandra was forty-nine years and surviving what had evolved into a tumultuous seventeen years marriage with Sean, husband of two wives, and a potential litany of unknown others, with three children of their own. The teenage children had more financial demands and did not crave the constant presence of their father as the young 5 years old one did. Sean was out and away more and more up to three months at a time, making money to maintain his luxurious lifestyle and provide for his family. He's lived by the principle "the ends serve the means." He believed there was a God and that He had blessed him although he was the architect of his success.

Xandra reached the turn off to the airport and curved along the road leading to the covered parking. She was one hour early. She stepped out of the car, then leaned in to retrieve her bag and novel. She removed her phone and purse then walked back to the boot and popped it open. She was about to bend into the boot to rearrange the shopping bags to leave space for Sean. She started to sigh, at the thought of his comment if he would see this. Her half-sigh ended in a choked gasp as her bag was pulled over her should and arm was twisted to her back. She saw a glistening point of the knife as was moved to press cold and sharp against the pulse of her throat. Fear screamed in her head and shrieked to her throat but before she could let it out, she was twisted around, and shoved towards the boot. She felt her vision blurring. "Please, let me go and take the bags. There is cash there. You can have the car if you wish." She pleaded. He loosed her hand and moved to jam his knife on one of the rear tires, and she ran as fast as her wobbly legs could take her. There were airport attendants not far away but she could only flail her hands and her voice did not come out. She walked up to one airport valet and grabbed him by the hand saying, "I have just been robbed in the parking and my car is still unlocked." "Are you sure? Where did that happen? Was it just now?" All she could do was nod as she walked him to the car. The boot was still open and the car unlocked but the guy was gone with her handbag. In her hand were the keys but the book and phone were still in the boot. "Thank you for coming with me." She said as she closed the boot and locked the car. "You should have screamed. What is in your bag? Let us go to security and alert them" "My passport and wallet. Thank God I am alive. I will not be able to pursue this further because I do not expect to get my bag back but only to ensure that there is more security in such dark parking." She was still breathing heavily and feeling weak in the joints as the proceed to the airport security office.

What Xandra needed was to be on time to meet Sean at arrivals and she had at least forty minutes before the plane landed. It would then take one more hour for him to come out. After making a statement at the security office, she proceeded to the arrivals to sit and collect her thoughts and read her novel. Her thoughts kept running to the incident, then the tasks she had not accomplished at home – things would elicit complaints and criticism. She wondered if Sean would love the food. It was always a ceremony when he arrived. He expected a big welcome first tea and chat, then a gourmet meal in a five-star diner setting. What Xandra would have preferred would be to eat out and be spoilt. He needed homemade food and if they did not accomplish it to expectation, she would suffer for it. Xandra was out of ideas and had ordered French beans with bacon bits, creamed spinach, rare steak with black pepper sauce, to compliment cumin fried rice and mash potato that she would make. She was going to pretend it was all made at home. Even though Sean was not big on dessert she had bought a fruit salad and vanilla ice cream. The rest of the days she would wing it. *"What do you serve a man who eats in hotels daily more than at home?"* She hated the anxiety it gave her, along with the sense of failure to satisfy Sean. Sadly, his open criticism had been in front of the children, and they believed him. Everything he rejected to eat the children would never eat either. Yet, her family and friends loved and praised her food. *"And what will say of my dress and hairstyle?"* She wondered.

She was woken up from her reveries as passengers started to arrive through the sliding automated doors, Xandra stood up and inched closer. Ten minutes later, she spotted Sean walking out pushing a trolley with large bags and duty-free parcels on top. She no longer felt the excitement at his arrival, but a relief to share some responsibilities like decision-making and school runs.

Sean stopped, moved to the side of the trolley, and hugged her. His arms and hands always felt good. He also smelt great. He pulled back a little with his left arm still around her waist and raised her face with his fingers on her chin, scrutinizing it. His fingers moved to caress her neck. He had seen the bruise. "What happened here? Did you get into a fight?" he enquired sounding alarmed. Xandra felt vulnerable as she recounted "I was accosted by a guy in the parking downstairs, and he took my bag. That mark is his knife." Even as she told him, she wondered if he would have been relieved if she had died. That thought shocked her too. "Were you not being security conscious? Were you making friends again?" Sean asked. That stung but she knew that she was very friendly to strangers, but she was security trained and cautious, which is a fact he knew. "I did not see where he came from as I went to check the boot. When I parked there was no one around, not even the valets." "I am so sorry darling," he said as he looked into her face again." Xandra smiled and looked away wanting to end that conversation. She grabbed his trolley and led him to the lifts. *"It is always my fault when bad things happen to me. No goodwill. No togetherness. No desire to protect. No partnership."*

Xandra decided it was best to explore the first Peter chapter three option for now. But nothing she ever did would satisfy her husband, how was she to win him to salvation by her conduct? She felt like a martyr. The only thing he did not criticize was sex. He was gentle with her, ensuring to attend to her satisfaction and for that alone she did not feel mishandled even if she felt used. The compromise had begun, and she had found scripture to support it besides Paul's instructions to "Do not deprive each other except perhaps by mutual consent and for a time, so that you may devote yourselves to prayer. Then come together again so that Satan will not tempt you because of your lack of self-control. 1 Corinthians 7:5"; which she had obeyed for seventeen years, in sickness and in health.

Nothing changed. Sean and Xandra were doing the same thing over and over again and getting the same results. They both seemed to want out but were not ready to let go.

30

God, the Master, The Holy of Israel, has this solemn counsel: "Your salvation requires you to turn back to me and stop your silly efforts to save yourselves. Your strength will come from settling down in complete dependence on me— The very thing you've been unwilling to do. You've said, 'Nothing doing! We'll rush off on horseback!' You'll rush off, all right! Just not far enough! You've said, 'We'll ride off on fast horses!' Do you think your pursuers ride old nags? - Isaiah 30:15-17 MSG

"I feel like a dog chasing its tail. If dad were alive, he would say, 'only a dog returns to its vomit'" What did I expect? Xandra reprimanded herself. A thought occurred to her to look for counseling or another healing retreat.

An hour before she was due to start the school rounds to pick up the children, she visited the Hope Centre to ask for help. "Do you prefer individual counseling or group counseling? We have "Grace-filled Relationships: When good relationships go bad." Sue Wells asked. "I would certainly love to attend group counseling and hear how others are coping with relationships." "Well then here is a pamphlet on the contents and the forms to sign up. You are in favor too because it is the first group counseling course, it free. It starts on Friday evening, and a full day." "God loves me! I shall scan and send these forms back. Thank you, Sue. I shall see you on Friday evening."

31

Grace-filled or Cursefilled Relationship?

"Immediately, something like scales fell from Saul's eyes, and he could
see again. He got up and was baptized, "- Acts 9:18 NIV

Xandra woke up excited to go to the meeting she made lunch and diner and snacks for the children before she left for her session. She could not fix her problems herself, maybe she will figure it out this time. It is also a relief to admit her failures, bring the walls down around her shame. She got to the Hope Centre one hour early so she could settle her anxiety and help Sue. The chairs were arranged in a circle and cards were only first name. Five other ladies were standing around, not talking to each other but each was holding a paper cup of either tea or coffee. Xandra walked around greeting each one of them and not making talk in case they were feeling inhibited.

"I am Sue Wells, your counselor. Welcome courageous ladies. We shall start every session with prayer. *Holy Father, all glory, honor, and praise are Yours today. We, Your children come together to seek healing by Your principles, according to Your Word. Holy Spirit, please lead and guide us today and the days to come. Give us wisdom, discernment, obedience, and courage. Dispel all emotions and thoughts that do not glorify you and help us to be authentic here and hereafter. In the name of Jesus Christ, we pray. Amen."*

Sue opened her eyes and started working the presentation on the laptop. "We are all here to seek a solution to acknowledge problems that plague us, find the root cause of the problem, you with find encourage in dealing with the symptoms, find a prescription for the actions that need to be taken and ensure to never give up until we find peace, healing, and restoration. This is the first group counseling that we have held at this center. You have all signed a confidentiality agreement because just as you would want to be protected, you are expected to protect the others. We are in an environment of voluntary vulnerability to each other and must collaborate with respect, order, and dignity. You may vent your feelings in an orderly manner. What is shared in the group stays in the group? First, let us pray, then I can get to know each other then I shall lead us into the format of our forum. Please introduce yourselves and give us a little background about you: challenges, needs and, expected outcomes".

I am Lenka de Beer, unhappily married for 27 years and blessed with four sons, 21, 19, 17, and 15 years. I am a beautician, running a beauty parlor. My husband is a Banker. I suffer anxiety and ulcers because my husband has been very controlling. He has a terrible temper which gets worse over the years. It started with criticism of how I talked, what I said with our visitors and it spiraled to an inquisition about where I went and who I met. Occasionally he has hit me in the presence of our children, but his parents do not believe me. He calls me ugly, useless, fat, and has refused me my conjugal rights for three years. These verbal attacks cut deeper than the glass and plates he had thrown at me. He refuses to see anything wrong with him and will not change. On the other hand, I zeroed out my needs and personality; worked hard to please him, and lived only to perform right. I have, ever since we got married, derived my sense of well-being from his approval and satisfaction. I cannot go on like that anymore." Suppressing a sob, she went silent.

"I am Kunda Kentane. I am a businesswoman in dealing with women's and children's apparel. I support and fund my husband's business ventures. My experience is just about the same, except that I have been married 13 years with no children. My husband has been unfaithful from the moment we said our vows. I kept hoping that he would change when I give him children. I have occasionally caught and confronted him about his infidelities and obsession with pornography and he is not apologetic about it. Instead, he finds reasons to criticize, mock, and shame me about my looks and barrenness. When I confront him with his behavior, he brings up incidents from the past, and it seems he is holding onto them for a practical purpose. Once he gets onto that tangent, I retreat to avoid getting hurt further. He has taken to accusing me of having an affair too, not respecting him and not taking good care of him. Funny, when I met him he was hanging out with philandering friends and he seemed to have a roving eye. I assumed I was enough for him and would change him. I have to make a decision to let him go, or rather than kill myself with worry, if I can't find a way to change him. I knew a lady who after over 20 years of marriage was found dead in her home – poisoned herself. Her husband who had been nasty and lording it over her wept bitterly in loud regret. It was too late for her to hear it." She grimaced resignedly. There was an air of commiseration or identification with her pain.

Xandra who was sitting next to Kunda squirmed and said "I am Xandra Rafiq, a humanitarian, formerly working with United Nations but quit to raise my family. I have three beautiful children, two teenagers, and one little girl. My husband is a businessman. I do not know what has already been said that I haven't experienced. He was and is still a generous provider. I believe we were equally yoked when we met because we both walked in the flesh," she laughed. "I have since grown spiritually and with that, we have grown further apart. It shames me to think that I have tolerated a relationship that abased and shamed me so much. Besides what Kunda said, I agreed to marry a very attractive man who said he was separated from children. I foolishly believed and got engaged to him, then he made me his customary wife. I got to find out that I was not the only wife he had. Seventeen years later he had no intention of divorcing his first wife, and his other wife had two children, lived with him someplace when he was not with us. Because of his abusive stance, I stopped arguing or confronting him about anything and worked to survive him. He had the power to make me happy or miserable and I felt caged. I reacted to control the situation by working harder at changing myself and improving on service, but he kept raising the bar. Since my sense of wellbeing came from performance and his comfort, his words and actions had the power to indict me. I gave up my career to raise our family and now struggling to get the confidence to start afresh. He does not allow me to seek employment. At first, loved everything about me and praised me. I was never much of a cook and did not even want to be a stay-at-home wife but I was convinced that I would be taken care of. And he did for a few years. I was hoodwinked into believing that he was honest and chaste and protective of me. He turned out to be obsessed with pornography, serially unfaithful, critical of everything I did including the way I talk on the phone, the colors I love, my hobbies, my friends, my food, my care for his clothes, my fasting, and prayer and even Bible reading. When I confronted him about his infidelities, he threatened to beat me. He brought presents from women he had dated on his trips. He has tried to discourage our children from going to church, alienated them from the families that support and love us. He used many abusive words on me. I have been under seventeen years of emotional, mental, and once, physical abuse. I have prayed, engaged in spiritual warfare, sought advice, and prayed ceaselessly, given it my all. I desire to keep the peace for now and find a way to exit this relationship with my children but lack the financial means to do that. If I speak my mind, he could starve us or take my children from me. Something has to give, or my life is not worth anything." She stared at the empty paper cup in silence.

Hanna, raised her hand to indicate she was taking her turn then put it down saying "I'm Hanna Thompson, a qualified high school teacher. My husband is a Pastor at Life Church in Centurion. He is a good man but very authoritative. He beats me down with scripture to justify his dominance. He behaves like he is beyond reproach and has a scripture for every one of my failures. I am unemployed, at first by choice but never allowed to seek employment thereafter. We have been married for twelve years with three girls. Until I listened to Kunda, Xandra, and Lenka, I felt responsible for everything that has happened to me. I believed what I was told that I was inadequate in every way that counts as a wife and mother. He takes every opportunity to pour shame on me for something as small as forgetting to put the saltshaker at the table. He is the perfect and valuable one while I am the defective, useless, unfit mother. He concludes every verbal assault with 'what kind of a Pastor's wife are you anyway?' I do not recognize the man I loved and married, the father of my daughters. Every time I ask for permission to get a job, he tells me not to waste his time but give him a son or else he will find someone else to give him an heir. His children have to dress up in a certain way for his image. I have to wait on him hand and foot. If I give anyone else attention that makes me a slut, especially if I hug an acquaintance, family friend, or anyone. If I laugh with the girls, I am accused of giggling like a little one. I feel ugly, stupid, and rejected. Short of choking him, I need a way out. It feels like God listens to him more than I because he is His servant. Even my family and his family do not believe me because he is outwardly charming and gentle, seemingly righteous."

Suppressing tears and with a shaky voice, Refilwe pointed at her chest, "Refilwe Nene, employed by City of Tshwane in the Transport department. My husband works with the Municipality in the Utilities Department. I am so sorry to hear what you all are going through. I have experienced what all of you have been through. I have four children: two boys aged twenty-five, twenty-three years and two girls aged, twenty-one and nineteen years old. It breaks my heart that one loves a man and believes in him, then wakes up with a master, prisoner, brute, cheat, and liar. It makes me angry too!" She choked on a sob. Sue crossed the room and offered her a box. Sometimes I do not even like the man I married. I do not know if I still love him anyway. He has treated me in a way only my enemy would. He has torn my heart out, called me the ugliest things, and lied about me to my children. I am under constant scrutiny from him and my daughters who, seeking not to be victimized and desiring his affection have taken his side. The home and family I have created to be safe has become the least safe for me. He has confessed his infidelity to the girls. One of them came to confide in me and asked me not to give her away. I have taken to being defensive to fend off the constant indictment. I maintain an air of indifference and being right even when I am wrong. My children do not know how I feel because I wanted to protect them. I am not blameless though. I have learned that it is sometimes better to attack him first to disarm him. I dare not let my guard down and so I maintain a distance emotionally and physically. We still share the bed like two icicles. It exhausts my mind to even recount it all. Someone had better come up with a more colorful story." She giggled as she threw her head back letting her braids flow behind her back.

"My name is Tessa Burger, a pediatrician. My husband is a career diplomat. We returned from a tour of duty two years ago. It has been difficult to work because we moved a lot." She stopped and smiled looking around at all the other girls. "I thought I was cursed or bewitched to bear with the nonsense in our relationship. When I met him, he was divorced but intimate friends with his ex. He is also still friends with his ex-girlfriends. My husband is twelve years older than I and professes to be a Christian. How good a Christian, I let God be the judge. We have been married for five years and have three small children. My parents warned me to take my time and learn his ways before marrying him; and I thought they were not with the times. My closest friends told me that they sensed he was jealous and controlling and I should find out what exactly transpired in his past relationships. I was in love and refused to even consider that. He has slept with our maids, beaten me up, verbally insulted me in the presence of our children, and shamed me in the presence of visitors with criticism. I cannot understand the 1 Corinthians 13 kind of love because how can I not keep count of wrongs? How can I bear all things in love?" I thought that I would make him happy because I was loving, raised in a loving family with enough training to meet his needs. I do not feel love for him anymore, which, makes me feel guilty." Whenever I pack my belongings to leave, he reminds me that I am supposed to be a Christian, what have I been praying for? Is it I who has prayed poorly or is God rejecting my prayers? There has to be something I am missing, or sin blocking my prayers." She paused and gesticulated with her hand in the air, then changed her mind "that will be all for now.

"Sadly, when most people hear of abuse, they have an image of physically battered women. They do not realize that the abuse of the soul with words and emotional torment is deeper, more painful, and takes longer to heal. It is a murder of the soul. You have done well to acknowledge your problems and that is a great start. Let us take a break and stretch for 10 minutes then resume. I would like you to give you teaching about identity, to get to the root of the problem."

By the end of the last session, it was clear that none of the participants walked in their true identity – the identity in Christ. Whereas some found their identity in their career achievements, others found it in being someone's wife, and others in the social status and prestige of their family. That is why they were all so messed up: trapped, indicted, responsible, exposed, and defensive. They were in idolatrous relationships with their identity and eyes on their husbands and none of God.

They had to control their behaviors, to control their others' opinions of themselves ultimately trying to control others and the outcome of the relationships. This originated with Adam and Even who took their eyes off God as the primary source. This curse now plays out in human relationships as a result of the very same mistake. Husbands and wives making demands of each other as if he/she were the source rather than the resource. Worshipping the created rather than the creator. The curse God put on the woman in Genesis 3:16 NIV, saying "And you will desire to control your husband, but he will rule over you" was still playing itself out.

Xandra got home more exhausted from the emotions that arose while they shared of their miseries. Negative talk is heavy on the brain and soul. She could not wait to hear more, mainly to understand what her part was in this miserable relationship.

Saturday morning found the group more confident, curious, and inhibited. *"Something happens when one lets the walls down and allows oneself to become vulnerable, even with strangers."* Xandra thought. Sue got everyone seated with little effort and all attention was on the video teaching she was sharing 'Grace-filled or Curse-filled Relationship'. The facilitator explained the characteristics of a curse-filled relationship as controlling, unforgiving, reactive, shaming, and ego-driven. He went on to confirm to the eager hearers that this kind of relationship gets one "Tired" in the sense of feeling trapped, indicted, deceptively responsible, shamefully exposed, and vehemently defensive. Xandra was amazed that this facilitator was indicating what each of them had felt. She looked around and found the others shaking and nodding and some making notes furiously. Sue must have sensed the effect of this, and she paused the video. "Does any of you identify with what Professor Cross is saying?" There were a lot of murmurs in agreement and when she sat down, everyone was eager to continue. Some elements of the teaching touched on concepts Xanda had not thought of. Like the emptiness one feels overtime, feeling defective and ashamed because of pressure to maintain a dignified façade to the public, pressure for outward conformity with no loving empowerment for true, lasting, inner growth and change. A no-win situation, where working harder sets one up for further failure. The concept of performance affirmed where one has to perform to earn love and acceptance which in turn reaffirms one's value. The emptiness of the soul that keeps us wanting more, in search of life and worth. *"I cringe to think that I am in an idolatrous relationship with Sean where my well-being is dependent upon his approval."* Professor Cross explained what the ladies had already felt but needed to confirm that there were courses one took which proved detrimental too: denying the problem, fixing the other person, and fixing yourself. He concluded this session with "human beings have to resist the impulse to idolatry, the desire to draw their inner peace and well-being from something or someone other than Jesus Christ. Many husbands and wives are in the perpetual cycle of struggling to fix their broken gods. Thus, they fix what is broken." At the end of this teaching, each participant was given forms to help them identify the thought processes, events, and beliefs that caused them to end up in a curse-filled relationship.

Sue opened this session with a scripture reading from Romans 1:12 NIV, "that is, that you and

I may be mutually encouraged by each other's faith.." When she closed the Bible she announced "I have learned from a great mentor, that marriages do not fail because of lack of love, but lack of grace. Let us now listen to teaching on grace-filled relationships."

The facilitator of the teaching, Dr. Barlow explained that first and foremost, God requires each one to be in the right relationship with him. Secondly, the spouses should know their identity in Christ and that Christ alone is to define them. Third, spouses should be equally yoked. Fourth, they should perform under grace does not grind, for the audience of one, Jesus Christ. In his words: "it is grace that can make a good marriage into a great marriage. It is grace that restores intimacy, fosters forgiveness, and mends broken marriages. Grace is given to one who desperately needs it but does not deserve it." Xandra made good notes. If things have gone wrong in a relationship, one person cannot change the circumstances by changing themselves or the other but by turning the focus to the creator of marriage. On hearing this and feeling irritated she raised her hand and Sue paused the video. "How about the years that I prayed to God to make things right? We are hearing about what we should have done. I started off building my marriage on the sand and we were equally yoked when we met. What is one to do when it all fails?" Resting both her hands on her head she stopped. The other ladies wriggled in their seats. Sue smiled "give Dr. Barlow a chance to explain how it should be when it goes wrong and what to do about it." Xandra listened quietly, making notes on only that which was new to her.

"Man is commanded to love his wife, then the loved wife will submit freely and willingly. If a man is not under the LORDSHIP of Jesus Christ, it will take divine intervention to keep a united relationship." She brightened up when she heard "Each spouse should strive to meet the other's three inner needs of the heart being securely love, having significant purpose and retaining hope give spouse four vital freedoms: the freedom to be different, freedom to be vulnerable, freedom to be candid, and, freedom to make mistakes. Both spouses should learn how to resolve conflict and could attain mind-blowing sex through grace. The grace of God untethers hearts from attitudes and practices that encumber love, steal joy, and stifle potential. *"I am so tired of theories that keep me thinking I have to do something or that I missed something. I wonder if this man understands what it is like to do everything to make things work and fail."* Xandra fidgeted with her pen and notebook.

Thank God, it is a complimentary session. I want to hear of testimonies of those who have been where we, six have been and survived, succeeded, or exited. It reminds me of those nuns that I knew at school who got pregnant after making vows of chastity and then their lives went downhill after expulsion. It is like a curse covered them and even their hair and dress did not make them shine as the habit that was disrobed from them. I do not want to come of marriage looking like that." She stood up and exited to the foyer and walked out to the garden. She skipped the tea break and returned in time for the next session.

Sue passed out work papers requiring participants to write down what insights they had gathered from the first session. Noting that there was not much writing, she got back and started to teach that "God designed marriage to be a relationship through which spouses could covenant to experience companionship, physical relationship, respect, love, and caring. Abuse and neglect are condemned by Scripture and can break the marriage covenant. When a marriage covenant is broken, divorce is permitted, due to the hard-heartedness of the abuse. Divorce provides legal protection for the abused. Nevertheless, in the face of abuse, divorce is a complex decision that one has to make personally without outside influence because it is as painful as the loss through death. It requires physical, spiritual, and emotional support. One could first seek out scriptural guidelines for conflict resolution aiming at seeking reconciliation and advocacy, provide safety for the abused women and their children" There was an air of excitement, Hanna stood up clapping "Amen!" It seems she had found a connection and breakthrough with someone acknowledging a way out. Sue brightened up "God's covenantal design for marriage is broken by abuse, and although scripture does not give a direct mandate to divorce, it does not mandate that an abused wife must remain married to an abuser. We, the body of Christ are called to model God's compassion toward abused women through effective strategies designed to meet the needs of women who are trying to escape abusive relationships and that is what the Hope Centre is trying to achieve today. Now that you know your identity and what your rights are, let us complete the teaching of Dr. Barlow so we can put our heads together to figure out a way forward."

Xandra took camera shots of the presentation because she could not write as fast as the notes she wanted to take. "*Dr. Barlow is speaking to my heart at last*" The session ended on a high note and a one-hour break to list the lessons learned and strategize the way forward was scheduled in an hour. The next session started with each participant sharing what they heard from the teachings.

Tessa raised her hand, "I believe that God must have known that the marriage covenant would be challenged so that He made laws to protect all human beings and their slaves. So, if the Lord describes the man's companion as his *wife by covenant* and warns him not to deal treacherously with her. Read Malachi 2:14-15. Why is God letting these men get away with such maleficence? Understand that the man is obligated to be faithful to the covenant by being a provider of his wife's physical needs, protection of her reputation, and protection from abuse by all including herself. Therefore, this abuse and neglect break the covenant by the very person who is supposed to fulfill it. Accordingly, in Deuteronomy 22:10, the husband was fined for publicly defaming his wife, and Exodus 21 established penalties for personal injuries. It makes me mad that I have had to bear my end of the bargain and pay for it."

"Besides, abuse perverts the image of God. Instead of nurturing, sustaining, and enhancing a wife's God-given craving for love and affection, physical abuse distorts God's image of responsible dominion in a most destructive way. Neglecting to provide for a wife's physical needs distorts God's functional image to care for His creation. Thus, a man who neglects to provide for the needs of his household is described as one who has "denied the faith and is worse than an unbeliever" as Paul says in 1 Timothy 5:8 NIV. I plan to shake my fists at the image bearer in my home to point that out if it will scare him in the least." Hanna laughed nervously.

"My husband thinks God gave him the mouth to insult me and our children whereas verbal abuse distorts God's image by failing to create life through words. That man thinks he is the creator of the whole family. I have constantly reminded him that Jesus said we would account for every careless word we speak. It gets him to shut up for a short while, but I guess his brain cannot switch off. I wonder if he can process that God is the creator, and death and life are in the power of the tongue; or that a soothing tongue is a tree of life, but perversion in it crushes the spirit. I shall refer him to the Proverbs 15:14. I am pleased to be reminded that each person is an image of God, to be respected, protected, and actively loved." Refilwe brought her hand to her mouth thoughtfully.

"My ladies in recovery, remember what Dr. Barlow said, that we are enough as we are. You are enough as you are! You do not need to perform for anybody ever again, but the LORD Jesus be your audience. I have learned today that the only pressure I should feel is the pressure of competing with the best version of myself. I do not need to change on demand to please someone else and no one needs to change for me. I shall follow advice to pause and rewrite the script that has been written by my husband and others for me; to define myself and seek what fulfills me and pleases the LORD. I commit to being intentional about not being angry. Anger is pain expressing itself. We must forgive and not allow people to take up residence free in your mind and stop your blessings. Hey! Not to judge either. Remember we are complicit in this union, and we might be causing some of the behavior even if we do not deserve the abuse." Confident Kunda raised her fists in the air. All the girls in unison with fists in the air chorused, "girl power!"

"That's a very good point, Kunda. Let God be the judge. Let God be your vindicator and avenger. Your only responsibility is to courageously stand against abuse." Sue interjected then called everyone to stand and stretch. As they sat down, Lenka quipped, "We have heard and know all these, but when push gets to shove, who will stand? Fear tends to win when one is financially dependent." She paused as if debating with herself. "That's it! I know that fear is the absence of faith. One has to trust that if we stand, God will fight for us. If we lose our lives, we can be rewarded for trusting and being courageous. These men know our deepest fears because we have been dependent on them. There are a lot of things to do out there but fear and worry and chronic abuse make me feel stupid, caged, and incapable of anything. We have to be ready to be martyred." She giggled and the others joined in. With a serious tone, Lenka launched as if voicing her thoughts aloud "The LORD is my shepherd I shall not lack for food. God's plans for us are to prosper not for calamity, to give us hope and a future. No weapon formed against me shall prosper. In God, I have put my trust, what can man do to me. Fight fear with faith. Here is another interesting angle, Dr. Barlow mentioned Isaiah 61:1 which Jesus quoted as His mission; that He was sent to give comfort to the brokenhearted, and to proclaim that captives are released and prisoners will be free. Surely, God wants us to stand strong, fearless, and courageous because Jesus already died for us to be free. If we accept to be abused, manipulated, intimidated, held at ransom because of finances and fear of losing our children then our Savior died for nothing. Will not the savior of the world vindicate, provide and fulfill His promise? I am resolved to stake my life on this assurance. I shall no longer be made to feel like a useless, outcast. He can hurl every insult at me but I will not take offense and if he touches me I shall have him arrested. Enough hypocrisy! Let us walk and live like the victorious Christians that Jesus died for. I am a child of God, evil will not touch me. No wonder we pray and get no results – professing faith we pray in fear and doubt that we are deserving of the break. When all along, Paul taught that you have adorned the spiritual armor, pray and when you have done all, to stand. Stand your ground as the redeemed of the LORD." This was a major revelation for all, including Lenka and Sue. Xandra, Tessa, and Hanna burst into tears. For what seemed like ten minutes they let flow the frustration, anger, joy of revelation, exasperation, unanswered prayers, fear, bitterness, weaknesses, losses and suppressed feelings they probably could not express.

"Thank you, Lenka, for that insight. We must resist the devil. Resist his wiles of oppression, intimidation, control, and protect your faith and the children. They are watching us and judging how we handle relationships. Are we telling them to let themselves be treated like doormats? Are we raising our sons to think that God allows women to be mistreated or protected? Are we going to let our children think marriage is a sinkhole and not a covenant that God designed to last forever? Their little hearts are breaking too. They see themselves as half of each parent therefore trashing one breaks half of them. We must put works to our faith." Xandra asked and pleaded in between sobs. "Whatever we do, we must protect the children from split loyalties and manipulation, scapegoating, and gaslighting.

"I would like to share a piece of advice a confidant gave me, and it worked wonders. Be blameless in your words and actions. Do not talk unnecessarily, respond, defend, or overexplain yourself each time you are confronted because there is power in silence. Secondly, do things differently to please you and your children. Do not show anger or hurt or exasperation or accept the blame. Just zone out when you sense aggression in words or actions. If you must, respond to threats, verbal abuse, criticism, or accusation, use the word of God, not yours. If you are threatened with harm, go and make a police report and keep a report with a friend or lawyer. You need to announce to the one who has threatened that you have informed your family and friends of such a threat. Avoid crying on many shoulders because when it is all over you will have undressed yourself and the father of your children. Long after you have forgiven him, the others might still bear a grudge. Lastly, do not listen to the fear and expectations of others. You decide what to make of your life and that of the children. Lastly, if you find out that some of your friends judge you, do not take offense after all you have them the material to work with. Your plight might be heavy, long, and burdensome for some people such that they are forced to confide in others." Xandra advised authoritatively.

The best highlight of the counseling session to all was the finale. Sue admonished "You have to submit and call upon Holy Spirit to come, take over and help you because if you have done all that you know how to do and have come to the end of yourself, you need divine intervention. You stand. Remember to face your pride and dethrone it because, just like fear, it clouds your thinking and makes your soul do what the spirit does not agree with. Jesus decided what was most important and died for it. You too will make sacrifices for what matters most. What matters most to each one of you may differ at various stages of your life. But you have to make up your mind. You are hanging onto a person that came declaring good intentions but is now holding your happiness captive. 2 Timothy 3:6-7 NIV tells *us 'They are the kind who worm their way into homes and gain control over gullible women, who are loaded down with sins and are swayed by all kinds of evil desires, 7 always learning but never able to come to a knowledge of the truth'."* You could hear a pin drop as Sue paused to let that sink in. "You will not make important decisions until you hit rock bottom, are threatened with the loss of what matters most, are suffocating under the load, and have no way out but to push back. At that stage, nothing else matters but to breathe."

"You might be saying to yourself, 'it will be painful? I cannot afford to take care of the children. I do not know where to start to rebuild my life. I do not want to lose the luxuries…" Sue squeaked. There was sighing all around. "There will be pains. There will be pain whether you stay or whether you leave. The pain of leaving is temporary while the pain for staying is indefinite. When you allow your soul and spirit to come into agreement, so you do not remain conflicted, being tossed back and forth. Paul prayed in 1 Thessalonians 5:23 NIV *'May God himself, the God of peace, sanctify you through and through. May your whole spirit, soul, and body be kept blameless at the coming of our Lord Jesus Christ. … And may your whole spirit, soul, and body be kept sound and blameless at the coming of our Lord Jesus Christ.* I say, suffering once and for all and own your pain, earn your freedom. As you harvest the fruit of courage and endurance which is freedom and peace. Forgive completely. It does not mean to compromise again but let God avenge and vindicate you. Do not confuse forgiveness and trust. Forgiveness is unconditional and a commandment while the trust is earned. I remind you of Apostle Peter's encouragement that *'And the God of all grace, who called you to his eternal glory in Christ, after you have suffered a little while, will himself restore you and make … (1 Peter 5:10 NIV).'"* Sue' voice rose a notch as she emphasized in conclusion, "The choice to stay implies that you will have the pain of wasted years later for choosing to stay with someone who does not value or build you up but tear you down. By the time you wake up to reality, all your youth will be gone, along with self-esteem and confidence, children's lives ruined, bitter from being robbed of opportunities to grow, expand, and be the best you were created to be. Is it worth it? Do you think that is God's plan and will for you? Whatever your decision, choose wisely. Commit it to the LORD and He alone will give you the desires of your heart."

32

"The unseen internal scars are uglier and deeper than those of wounds from physical assault. They are usually covered up too well as they etch deeper covered in glossy low self-esteem and the desperate need of the victim to maintain semblance of beauty, wellness and strength."

— Daphne Balinda

"Being heard, having pain acknowledged, and finding support with a way forward is very empowering. The lioness focuses right, regains her strength and God's warrior is unleashed. I look forward to our follow up session in a month," smiled Xandra as she drove home.

"Mommy mommy, guess who is here?" Her heart fluttered for a moment and she started to pray *"LORD who closed the lion's mouth to save Daniel, please close Sean's mouth."* We heard the gate bell ring and saw a car outside, then daddy was just there!" "Oh baby, I see how happy you are. Your prayers have been answered. Isn't that great?" Xandra's eyes widened as she bent to kiss Zoe, feigning excitement.

As Xandra ascended the stairs towards the bedrooms, Sean walked into the corridor from his bedroom and glared at her. "Welcome home." "Yeah! To an empty house. The woman is gone leaving the children unattended." She unsmilingly stopped in front of him and extended a greeting hand. Sean looked at her hand, sneered, and walked past her to the family lounge. *"If only I were strong enough I would box him in the mouth by surprise,"* Xandra smiled at the thought and the shocked reaction it would elicit, as walked on to the bedroom that she had moved into, belonging to Zoe, her youngest child. She put her bag down, took off her shoes, and walked out to go and greet the children who were by now huddling around their dad. The children looked up to her warily torn between joy at seeing her and fear of antagonizing their father. Xandra walked up to each one of them and kissed them on the forehead and walked out.

Dinner was filled with chattering of the children while Sean and Xandra neither exchanged a word nor look. The children chattered happily and a lot to share, jokes and riddles too. Xandra genuinely enjoyed their camaraderie, exclaimed, responded to their stories and questions while Sean was silent as if intending to make them uncomfortable. *"Why did he come back if he is not coming in peace. How selfish not to make an effort to entertain and be civil for the sake of the children! We would not be sitting here if it was not for them."* Xandra resolved to do something she had not tried before. *"I shall give him a dose of his medicine. He will get my unsmiling face from now on. He cannot just switch temperament without consideration of others. He is not my friend; I will not try to be friendly but civil and amicable for this business of surviving each other as we raise the children. Soon enough he will be gone again, and we shall have fun."*

That night, the children did not watch television with her but followed their dad to the bedroom. They played and talked and fought amongst themselves as he pored over his laptop reading the news, neither listening nor giving them any attention. That night, Xandra watched the show "Who on Earth Did I Marry?" When she retired to bed, all scripture and good thoughts had evaporated and the tape that played in the head was of every nasty thing Sean had said to her. She remembered his reactions to things he should have apologized for but deflected and attacked her in criticism. She remembered how she had to plead and reason with him to let her go home to see her mother and sister in hospital whereas he would rush to go attend to his mother. All the injustices, bitter feelings, shame, self-deprecation came rushing out. She was angry and could not sleep. Past midnight, she heard her door latch move. Then she waited and heard a gentle knock. It was Sean. She knew what he wanted. *"what gull to treat me so and come knocking on the to wake her up? He is going to ask me to sleep with him, then beg, then rant and rave and finish with threatening. I have had it!"* She waited until he knocked again them, she pulled her prayer shawl around her shoulders and went to open the door. "I am praying. I cannot talk to you she said as she faced him." "I just want to tell you to come back to our room." "No Sean. I shall not come to the bedroom. I am going to pray and meditate all night." She walked towards her bed and fell to her knees. He surprised her by following and kneeling beside her. She chose to ignore him and bent her head in silence. After a long while, he got up "I am going to be waiting for you in bed. Xandra wanted to shout at him *"I am not your sex object. My body is not your possession"* but thought better of it because it would draw him into an argument that could last all night as before. She closed her bedroom door and went to sleep uncomfortably. *"This man will not talk to me in the daylight but will invade my space in the dark!"*

The breakfast was prepared by the housekeeper and although she had eaten earlier, she politely gave him company at the table, as was the custom. Sean did not raise his eyes to acknowledge her but ate quietly. As he poured himself a cup of tea, he looked at her sideways extended the flask to pour her a cup. Xandra accepted politely "Thank you." "Let us have a meeting when I get back this afternoon." "Sure" was all Xandra could say even as she dreaded that talk. There was a calm resolve that she had to take her power back at all costs.

33

"I believe that there will be ultimately be a clash between the oppressed and those who do the oppressing. I believe that there will be a clash between those who want freedom, justice and equality for everyone and those who want to continue the system of exploitation. I believe that there will be that kind of clash, but I don't think it will be based on the color of the skin..." — **Malcolm X**

"Xandra, we have three hours before picking up the children from school. Let us go talk away from home. I can buy you a beer." "Wait! Are you planning to treat me so you can come knocking on my door at night?" she enquired seriously and looked taken aback. Before he could answer she added, "that will not work you know?" "It is alright, I just want us to catch up and get on the same page." She already knew what she would hear so he had no positive expectations but had prepared her response. She closed her journal with an enthusiastic snap and leaned across the table with her eyes glowing with anticipation.

"Xandra, I do not understand how you deal with conflict. A man and his wife resolve their problems in bed. That is where all outstanding issues are successfully resolved. We cannot live together under the same roof under such conditions. You need to return to our bedroom and then we can resolve what issue you have against me. Any other will not work." Sean paused, Xandra kept silent watching him. My problems with you are the same throughout the years. You do not listen to me. I told you while we were courting that I cannot stand someone who does not listen." Xandra looked away wondering "*fancy trying to make peace with accusation and criticism.*" Sean murmured, "you have never given us the food we want. I stopped being bothered by that. You do not take care of my clothes. I stopped complaining about it. You go about hugging everyone and introducing new friends to us, that we have never met before. That I cannot accept. You fast and go for retreats without consulting with us. What sort of mother cooks for her family food that she does not eat? Last time you got up and decided you were going home to see your mother and I do not even believe she was sick, so I don't know why you decided without asking for permission. That was disrespectful. You do not respect me." At the last accusation, Xandra's temper rose because she had not recovered from his complaint that she did not first ask his permission to visit her sick mother. He noticed her agitation. "Do not raise your voice or interrupt me." He warned. He talked on for nearly an hour. Xandra had characteristically zoned out to protect her emotions. She checked out the other customers of the Karoo Café wondering about their personal lives and was intrigued by their choice of food. Sean enquired "would you like that beer after coffee?" "No thanks, I shall have hot water with lemon please." He looked at her disappointed. After giving the order for a drink. He turned around and stated "the ball is in your court, darling. You can make us all very happy or you can keep us all unhappy. Work on those things we ask for." He seemed done with his long list of grievances. Xandra summarized his message, calling his bluff, "as you say, I am worthless. I have failed to satisfy you as a wife and mother to our children. You are a special man Sean. You deserve better and that is why I recommend you carry on with your life. I am who I am and will not change into anything else. I have given it my all for seventeen years now and have failed to give you what you deserve." Sean was cornered and he started to protest but Xandra prompted him with "remember how you said that you do not your life to end up like you father, I believe you should make provision for that." There was no need to argue with him and he had their case well. She already knew that he had groomed a younger woman, that he had passed off as an orphaned foster child, with whom he had two young children. She was not going to raise the matter to deviate from the current state of affairs. The waiter arrived with the mug of hot lemon water, and Sean brusquely asked for the bill. "I was so happy you listened to me intently without interruption and hoped we would have more talks like this. We need to continue this discussion after diner." Sean still intrigued her. This time there was restrained violence and cruelty in him, an impression of wasted strength and cunning in his dancing eyes. He did not meet her gaze as he talked to her or listened to her. He only turned to look at her when she was not looking.

She found she was weeping. The tears poured down her face, and she could not stop them. Sean walked up beside her, and when he saw her tears, he stared straight ahead. "We shall be ok" he estimated thinking she was affected by the talk they had just had. "I was very happy while you courted me. I have wanted to run from you ever since I was seven months pregnant with our first child. I deliberately waited and hoped you would feel my love, accept me, and love me back. Now that it is over, I am relieved." She sobbed like her heart would flow out with the tears. Sean stood to attention as if woken up from a reverie. "Did we not just agree to try harder, change our ways, and make it work? What happened between the last hour and now?" "But that is the point. You made that assumption for both of us?" She laughed with guileless amusement. Sean raise his hands to her shoulders and turned her to him, searching her eyes. "What are you saying Xandra?" "That it is over between us. I no longer desire to be married. We have nothing in common. We are partners in raising our children and nothing more. I stayed on to raise this family, I am done. "But Xandra, have you thought this through? The children will be affected badly You are destroying our family! What sort of Christian are you? What do you pray? Are you taking advice from someone who is misleading you?" He fidgeted with the car keys as he looked away in the distance for a short while. With a raised voice he declared, "I am not afraid of you anymore". That confession that implied he was indeed afraid of her or had been was hilarious and surprising. *He has been afraid of me? Helpless, dependent, vulnerable me?*" Encouraged, she pointed out, "Sean, our children have been hurting for years. I know you love them as much as I do and will do everything to protect them. You are a good father, Sean, you will do what is best for them." She walked away with steady steps, head held high, feeling like her old self again." It felt so good to feel free, unafraid, and holding the reins of her future.

Sean did not turn up for diner. He was packing his bags. There was no knocking on her door that night. The children had sensed the mood and retired to their rooms right after diner. Zoe was breathing heavily next to Xandra. She lay in the darkness unable to sleep herself. There was too much to think about, too much planning to do, and she smiled at her thoughts. *"So, at last, the sword of power is in my hands - and we will see, with much thanks to God, who is the underdog now."* There would be counter-attack battles and possibly painful ones, but today, she was free of fear and owned her body and emotions. The battle belongs to the LORD and victory belongs to Jesus.

HER TOWER OF BABEL

Unless the LORD builds the house
the builders labor in vain.
Unless the LORD watches over the city,
the guards stand watch in vain.
[2] In vain you rise early and stay up late, toiling for food to eat
—for he grants sleep to[a] those he loves.
Psalm 127:1-3 NIV

CITATIONS

The Holy Bible. New International Version, Zondervan, 1984.

The Holy Bible: King James Version. Dallas, TX: Brown Books Publishing, 2004.

Peterson, Eugene H. *The Message: The Bible in Contemporary Language.* NavPress, 2002.

Tyndale House Publishers. (2004). *Holy Bible: New Living Translation.* Wheaton, Ill: Tyndale House Publishers.

Casey JR, Bob. *"I Was Heart Broken, Scared, I Had a Lot of Anxiety, I Was Worried, I Felt Weak, and I Had No Idea How I Was Ever Going to Come up with the Strength. But I Just Closed My Eyes, and Took a Blind Lean. I Knew I Had to Get out of There".*, www.quotefancy.com/bob-casey-jr-quotes. Accessed 16 June 2021.

Howitt, M. (1829). *"Will you walk into my parlor?" said the Spider to the Fly, "'Tis the prettiest little parlor that ever you did spy; The way into my parlor is up a winding stair, And I've a many curious things to shew when you are there."* Bec McMaster, Soulbound. https://www.goodreads.com/work/quotes/57757885-soulbound-dark-arts-3. Accessed 17 June 2021.

"Malcom X. *"I Believe That There Will Be Ultimately Be a Clash between the Oppressed and Those Who Do the Oppressing. I Believe That There Will Be a Clash between Those Who Want Freedom, Justice and Equality for Everyone and Those Who Want to Continue the System of Exploitation. I Believe That There Will Be That Kind of Clash, but I Don't Think It Will Be Based on the Color of the Skin...,"* www.goodreads.com/quotes/265023-i-believe-that-there-will-be-ultimately-be-a-clash. Accessed 16 June 2021.

Peck, Scott M. "The Road Less Traveled: A New Psychology of Love, Traditional Values and Spiritual Growth." *"Truth or Reality Is Avoided When It Is Painful. We Can Revise Our Maps Only*

When We Have the Discipline to Overcome That Pain. To Have Such Discipline, We Must Be Totally Dedicated to Truth. That Is to Say That We Must Always Hold Truth, as Best We Can Determine It, to Be More Important, More Vital to Our Self-Interest, than Our Comfort. Conversely, We Must Always Consider Our Personal Discomfort Relatively Unimportant and, Indeed, Even Welcome It in the Service of the Search for Truth. Mental Health Is an Ongoing Process of Dedication to Reality at All Costs.," 2 Jan. 1998, www.goodreads.com/quotes/8648608-truth-or-reality-is-avoided-when-it-is-painful-we.

Thurber, J. (n.d.). *"All men should strive to learn before they die, what they are running from, and to, and why."* Quotable Quote. Retrieved June 17, 2021, from https://www.goodreads.com/quotes/997787-all-men-should-strive-to-learn-before-they-die-what

Wilde, Oscar. "You Don't Love Someone for Their Looks, or Their Clothes, or for Their Fancy Car, but Because They Sing a Song Only You Can Hear.," www.goodreads.com/quotes/150419-you-don-t-love-someone-for-their-looks-or-their-clothes. Accessed 16 June 2021.

Ustinov, Peter. "The Point of Living and of Being an Optimist, Is to Be Foolish Enough to Believe the Best Is yet to Come," www.goodreads.com/quotes/361032-the-point-of-living-and-of-being-an-optimist-is. Accessed 16 June 2021.

Come live with me and be my love,
And we will all the pleasures prove,
That Valleys, groves, hills, and fields,

Woods, or steepy mountain yields", Marlowe, Christopher. "The Passionate Shepherd to His Love." "The Passionate Shepherd to His Love"., www.poetryfoundation.org/poems/44675/the-passionate-shepherd-to-his-love.

Accessed 16 June 2021.

"Even as the archer loves the arrow that flies, so too he loves the bow that remains constant in his hands." (n.d.). Nigerian Proverb. Retrieved June 17, 2021, from https://thoughtcatalog.com/kovie-biakolo/2014/12/25-ancient-african-proverbs-about-love-that-will-make-you-rethink-everything/

"The unseen internal scars are uglier and deeper than those of wounds from physical assault. They are usually covered up too well as they etch deeper covered in glossy low self-esteem and the desperate need of the victim to maintain semblance of beauty, wellness and strength." – Daphne Balinda

"A person's character is like pregnancy it cannot be hidden." (n.d.). African Proverb. Retrieved June 17, 2021, from https://www.inspirationalstories.com/proverbs/african-a-persons-character-is-like-pregnancy-it-cannot/

Love truth even if it hurts you. Hate lies, even if they help you. (n.d.). African Proverb. Retrieved June 17, 2021, from https://web.facebook.com/africanproverbspage/posts/african-proverb-love-truth-even-if-it-hurts-you-hate-lies-even-if-they-help-you-/4461150513958371/?_rdc=1&_rdr

"Do not throw away the oars before you reach the shore." (n.d.). African Proverb. Retrieved June 17, 2021, from https://www.inspirationalstories.com/proverbs/african-do-not-throw-away-the-oars-before-the/

Covey, Stephen. "Accountability Breeds Response-Ability." www.brainyquote.com/quotes/stephen_covey_636497 Accessed 16 June 2021.

Scott, Walter. "O, What a Tangled Web We Weave When First We Practise to Deceive!" O, What a Tangled Web We Weave When First We Practise to Deceive!, www.brainyquote.com/quotes/walter_scott_118003. Accessed 16 June 2021.

Emerson, Ralph Waldo. "'The Purpose of Life Is Not to Be Happy. It Is to Be Useful, to Be Honorable, to Be Compassionate, to Have It Make Some Difference That You Have Lived and Lived Well."

www.goodreads.com/quotes/64541-the-purpose-of-life-is-not-to-be-happy-it. Accessed 16 June 2021.

King, Stephen. "On Writing: A Memoir of the Craft." "Fool Me Once, Shame on You. Fool Me Twice, Shame on Me. Fool Me Three Times, Shame on Both of Us.," 2 June 2020, www.stephenking.com/works/nonfiction/on-writing-a-memoir-of-the-craft.html

Abdelnour, Ziad K. "Economic Warfare: Secrets of Wealth Creation in the Age of Welfare Politics." "Three Things You Cannot Recover in Life: The WORD after It's Said, the MOMENT after It's Missed and the TIME after It's Gone. Now You Know.," 2011, www.perlego.com/book/999730/economic-warfare-secrets-of-wealth-creation-in-the-age-of-welfare-politics-pdf.

"The Ayn Rand Lexicon: Objectivism from A to Z (Ayn Rand Library): Return to Compromise." "There Are Two Sides to Every Issue: One Side Is Right and the Other Is Wrong, but the Middle Is Always Evil.," 1 Jan. 1988, www.aynrandlexicon.com/lexicon/compromise/5.html

that you know how to do and have come to the end of yourself, you need divine intervention. You stand. Remember to face your pride and dethrone it because, just like fear, it clouds your thinking and makes your soul do what the spirit does not agree with. Jesus decided what was most important and died for it. You too will make sacrifices for what matters most. What matters most to each one of you may differ at various stages of your life. But you have to make up your mind. You are hanging onto a person that came declaring good intentions but is now holding your happiness captive. 2 Timothy 3:6-7 NIV tells *us 'They are the kind who worm their way into homes and gain control over gullible women, who are loaded down with sins and are swayed by all kinds of evil desires, 7 always learning but never able to come to a knowledge of the truth'."* You could hear a pin drop as Sue paused to let that sink in. "You will not make important decisions until you hit rock bottom, are threatened with the loss of what matters most, are suffocating under the load, and have no way out but to push back. At that stage, nothing else matters but to breathe."

"You might be saying to yourself, 'it will be painful? I cannot afford to take care of the children. I do not know where to start to rebuild my life. I do not want to lose the luxuries..." Sue squeaked. There was sighing all around. "There will be pains. There will be pain whether you stay or whether you leave. The pain of leaving is temporary while the pain for staying is indefinite. When you allow your soul and spirit to come into agreement, so you do not remain conflicted, being tossed back and forth. Paul prayed in 1 Thessalonians 5:23 NIV *'May God himself, the God of peace, sanctify you through and through. May your whole spirit, soul, and body be kept blameless at the coming of our Lord Jesus Christ. ... And may your whole spirit, soul, and body be kept sound and blameless at the coming of our Lord Jesus Christ.* I say, suffering once and for all and own your pain, earn your freedom. As you harvest the fruit of courage and endurance which is freedom and peace. Forgive completely. It does not mean to compromise again but let God avenge and vindicate you. Do not confuse forgiveness and trust. Forgiveness is unconditional and a commandment while the trust is earned. I remind you of Apostle Peter's encouragement that *'And the God of all grace, who called you to his eternal glory in Christ, after you have suffered a little while, will himself restore you and make ... (1 Peter 5:10 NIV).'"* Sue' voice rose a notch as she emphasized in conclusion, "The choice to stay implies that you will have the pain of wasted years later for choosing to stay with someone who does not value or build you up but tear you down. By the time you wake up to reality, all your youth will be gone, along with self-esteem and confidence, children's lives ruined, bitter from being robbed of opportunities to grow, expand, and be the best you were created to be. Is it worth it? Do you think that is God's plan and will for you? Whatever your decision, choose wisely. Commit it to the LORD and He alone will give you the desires of your heart."

AUTHOR'S NOTE

I ask my readers to remember that Her Tower of Babel is a work of fiction. The physical locations I mentioned do exist. The characters are fictitious. The experiences of the characters have been well-researched to be characteristic of dysfunctional marriages and abusive relationships.

ABOUT THE AUTHOR

Daphne Balinda Ketter is a Sociologist, Mompreneur, humanitarian, a Licensed Minister (https://www.christianleadersalliance.org/minister-directory/), Social Etiquette Coach, and a Blogger. She is a member of Moms in Prayer International, a member of the Christian Leaders Alliance.

She was born in Uganda, now residing with her family in South Africa. She is a Christian mother of two daughters, Danielle and Trudy, and a son, Arnold. She is a continuing student of the Christian Leaders Institute; holds a Bachelor of Arts Hons. degree in Sociology from the University of South Africa; a Bachelor of Science degree in Economics with Sociology specialism from the University of London, and a Diploma in Business Studies from Kensington College of Business. She is actively involved in Prayer and Evangelism Ministry; and a passionate advocate for youth and women empowerment.

Daphne felt a call to blog messages of encouragement. She intends to write books with spiritual overtones, communicating the message that faith in Jesus Christ brings freedom, emotional healing, and spiritual breakthrough. This book is her first venture in fiction. She is committed to making a difference in lives whenever, wherever, and however possible as a disciple of Jesus Christ. She has experienced much love, joy, and fulfillment alongside pain and poor decisions and falls in life. You can visit her blog where she encourages the weary. Visit her blog at https://graceandchivalry.wordpress.com/

Printed in the United States
by Baker & Taylor Publisher Services